A Question of Magic

Also by E.D. Baker

THE TALES OF THE FROG PRINCESS
The Frog Princess
Dragon's Breath
Once Upon a Curse
No Place for Magic
The Salamander Spell
The Dragon Princess

Fairy Wings
Fairy Lies

TALES OF THE WIDE-AWAKE PRINCESS
The Wide-Awake Princess
Unlocking the Spell

A Question of Magic

E.D. BAKER

BLOOMSBURY

LONDON NEW DELHI NEW YORK SYDNEY

Bloomsbury Publishing, London, New Delhi, New York and Sydney

First published in Great Britain in April 2014 by
Bloomsbury Publishing Plc
50 Bedford Square, London WC1B 3DP

First published in the USA in October 2013 by
Bloomsbury Children's Books
1385 Broadway, New York, New York 10018

www.bloomsbury.com
www.edbakerbooks.com

Bloomsbury is a registered trademark of Bloomsbury Publishing Plc

A CIP catalogue record for this book is available from the British Library

ISBN 978 1 4088 3929 4

Printed and bound in Great Britain by CPI Group (UK) Ltd, Croydon CR0 4YY

1 3 5 7 9 10 8 6 4 2

This book is dedicated to Kim, my inspired research assistant and my very own Baba Yaga. To Ellie, my future Baba Yaga, who is always up for some creative brainstorming. To Kevin, who knows the true answers to my computer questions. To my fans, who help me believe in myself. And to Victoria, who knows how to ask the right questions.

CHAPTER 1

Serafina watched as Alek folded the metal back on itself and used a heavy mallet to beat it flat once again. He was making a sword for Sir Ganya, a local knight who had promised more work if this piece turned out well. Serafina always enjoyed watching Alek, whether he was making horseshoes, nails, or something as refined as a sword. Although his father specialized in plows and axles and tools ordinary people needed, Alek preferred to work on items that required a more precise touch.

Alek's father, Kovar, grinned at Serafina from the other side of the blacksmith shop. Everyone knew that Serafina liked seeing how things were done. Her own father's nickname for her was Kitten because he swore that she was as curious as a cat. Whether she was watching someone work or asking questions about things she didn't understand, Serafina was always interested in learning something new.

"When you finish working on that sword for the day, you can help me take off the axle I'm fixing next," Alek's father told him. "The farmer who brought the wagon in wants it as soon as possible."

Alek nodded and wiped the sweat from his eyes. His father was a strong man, but Serafina had seen Alek lift almost as much weight.

"Miss Serafina! There you are!" Tasya, her mother's servant girl, waved at her from the doorway. "A letter came for you! Your mother wants you to come home now. Everyone is waiting for you to read it!"

Serafina's eyes went wide. A letter was always a big event, and she could imagine how excited her family must be. "I'll come back to tell you what it is as soon as I can," she told Alek.

He had been her best friend since they were children, but in the last few years he'd become something more. After her family, he would be the next person to hear any news she had to share.

* * *

Serafina was reaching for the door to her parents' house when it flew open and her sister stepped out. "There you are!" snapped Alina. "We've been waiting for you to come home."

"How are you?" Serafina asked her.

Alina rubbed her belly. "I think the baby will be here soon. I've been having little pains for the last few days. And look at my ankles!" she said, lifting the hem of her skirt. "They're so swollen I can't lace up my boots. Come into the kitchen. I need to sit down. Nesha Zloto is here," she added in a whisper. "The old gossip is in the kitchen with Mother and won't leave until you read the letter."

Serafina's father, Tadeo Divis, the most sought-after master builder in the town of Kamien Dom in the kingdom of Pazurskie, had encouraged his youngest daughter to learn to read and write. No one else in her family had been interested. After Serafina learned, she taught Alek and often shared her books with him.

Someone laughed inside the kitchen as Serafina followed Alina through the door. Their mother, Zita, was seated at the table across from a white-haired woman. Tasya had gone into the kitchen before the girls and was already pouring hot water into the teapot.

Zita's eyes lit up in a way that always made Serafina feel warm inside.

"Oh, good, you're here, Fina!" said Zita. "Tasya, I'll take care of the tea. I want you to run over to Katya's house and tell her that Fina is back."

Tasya set the pot on the table, wiped her hands on her apron, and hurried from the kitchen. Alina took a seat beside her mother and sighed.

Their neighbor, Widow Zloto, scowled when she glanced at the girls. "Alina can sit at the corner like that; just make sure you don't, Serafina. Move over! Alina is already married, so it won't affect her, but unmarried girls who sit at a corner will stay single for seven more years."

"Good day, Mistress Zloto," Serafina said, bending down to kiss the old woman's wrinkled cheek.

The widow Zloto patted Serafina's hand. "You can fetch me some of that good bread your mother makes, Fina."

"I'll have some, too," said Alina.

"I'll bring a plate to share," Serafina told them. She had already spotted the letter on the table, propped against a mug filled with daisies. Her fingers itched to pick up the letter, but instead she hurried to get the bread and cheese.

The bread was the traditional round loaf topped with salt usually given to guests and special company.

4

Her mother made one every day, knowing that at least one of the neighbors was bound to stop by.

"Don't forget the knife!" cried Widow Zloto. "It's bad luck to break bread with your hands. Break a loaf, break a life; that's what my mother used to say."

Serafina smiled. The old woman was one of the most superstitious people she knew, and she mentioned the knife every time she ate a piece of bread.

Alina leaned forward to rub the small of her back. "Hurry, Serafina! I want to hear your letter before this baby is born!"

"Your baby isn't coming this very minute," Widow Zloto told her. "But when it comes, you make sure no stranger sees it until it's at least two months old. It's bad luck if they do!" The sisters sang out along with the old woman, then laughed when she laughed, too. "So, I'm a little superstitious? What can I say, my mother was just as bad and my grandmother was even worse. But your sister is right, Serafina. Hurry so we can hear what's in the letter. I wonder who sent it."

Serafina couldn't imagine who might have written to her. Aside from her father, people in her family rarely received letters. When they did, everyone wanted to be there for the first reading. Because she and her father were the only ones in the family who knew how to read, they were often asked to read the letters over and over again. The few letters they did receive were usually their only connection with some of their friends and relatives and were generally treasured and set aside to keep.

Serafina's mind raced as she tried to think who might have sent *her* a letter. Could it be one of her cousins inviting her to visit? Perhaps it was her old friend Eva, whose family had moved away the year before. Serafina was pondering the possibilities as she carried the still-warm bread to the table.

The door opened and her oldest sister, Katya, burst into the kitchen, out of breath from running. "Oh, good! I'm not too late!" she said, collapsing into a chair. "Mother, the children were taking their naps, so I asked Tasya to stay and watch them. I hope you don't mind."

"Not at all," said Zita.

"It's good that Tasya won't be here," declared Widow Zloto. "Servants love to gossip. Whatever your letter says would be all over town before nightfall. I know— you should hear what my serving girl tells me!"

"You sit down now, Fina," said her mother. "Read the letter while I take care of the food. We can't stand the suspense any longer."

Serafina set the knife on the table, slid into her seat, reached for the letter, and turned it over in her hands.

She had hoped to see who had sent it, but the writing on the back simply said "Serafina Divis."

"What does it say?" Alina asked, leaning toward the table.

"Just my name," said Serafina. "No address or anything."

Even the stamp used to press the sealing wax had been plain, without the usual initial or decoration. Frowning in concentration, Serafina broke the wax and spread the letter open on the table.

"Don't start yet, Fina!" said Katya. "Let Mother sit down and get comfortable. I'm just sorry Father is away," she added. "He would love to hear the letter, I'm sure. All right. You can start now."

Serafina glanced from one person to the next. "Are you certain I can read it? No one has to fetch someone else or start supper or—"

"Just read the thing!" Alina ordered, kicking her leg under the table.

Serafina grinned, but her hands were shaking when she began.

> *Dear Serafina,*
> *I am sure you have never heard of me,*
> *but I am your great-aunt Sylanna from*

*your grandmother Yanamaria's side. I am
writing to inform you of the inheritance
that I intend to leave you. This
inheritance is of great importance and
will change your life forever. Should you be
interested in this bequest, come to the
town of Mala Kapusta on the next market
day. At nine o'clock that night, go to the
house located at the westernmost edge of
the town, past the Bialy Jelen tavern.*

*Looking forward to your arrival,
Your great-aunt Sylanna*

"She's right. I've never heard of her," said Alina. "Who is Sylanna? And why is she leaving anything to Fina? Why not me or Katya? We're older, after all. Mother, have you ever heard of this person?"

"The name isn't familiar, but then your grandmother had so many sisters. Some of them died young, others moved away."

"An inheritance!" said Widow Zloto. "Well, well! We might have a little heiress here! I do wonder why she chose you for this honor. Not that you aren't deserving, dear child, but your sisters have been completely cut out."

"It isn't fair!" complained Alina.

"I'm sure Great-Aunt Sylanna had a reason," said Katya. "But I can't imagine why she would pass over two older sisters for Fina."

"What do you suppose it is?" their mother mused.

"Money, of course," said Widow Zloto. "Inheriting a lot of money would change anyone's life."

"Perhaps it's a small business," said Katya. "Then she'd have to move to Mala Kapusta. It makes sense that she'd inherit that. Both Alina and I have families of our own and can't just pick up and leave."

"We won't know why I was named or what my inheritance is until I go to claim it," Serafina declared. "Do you think Father will be home in time to take me?"

Her mother shook her head. "He'll be gone for another week at least. The next market day is tomorrow."

"I wish Alek could go with me—but I know it wouldn't be proper, so I won't ask him," she hurried to say, even as her mother and Widow Zloto opened their mouths to protest. Serafina turned to Alina, but she knew the answer even before she asked. "I don't suppose that Yevhen—"

"He can't go anywhere! How can you ask with the baby coming so soon?"

"I know, I know. Plus he's busy taking inventory in

his father's warehouse," said Serafina. Alina's husband worked for his father, a successful wine merchant.

"Why doesn't Viktor take her?" asked Widow Zloto. "He's always so busy, but he can take a day off for that, surely?"

As one of her father's apprentices, Viktor had lived with the family for seven years, and then another two as a journeyman. Soon after receiving his master builder's certificate, he'd married Katya and they'd moved into their own small home.

Serafina had been just a little girl when Viktor had started his apprenticeship. On his first day there, she had caught him rifling through another apprentice's belongings. He was so good at lying, however, that no one believed her. After that, Viktor had shown that he didn't like her in lots of little ways, making fun of her when her parents weren't around, pulling her hair when no one was looking. Her favorite necklace went missing one day and turned up broken the next. Serafina was certain that Viktor had done it. Things hadn't gotten much better between them since.

"Of course Viktor can go," said Katya.

"But—" began Serafina.

"Then it's settled," said her mother. "You'll leave early in the morning and be there by supper time. I'm sure

Great-Aunt Sylanna will invite you to spend the night, and you can return the next day."

From the look in her mother's eye, Serafina knew there wasn't any point in arguing. She sat back as the women began to talk of other things, wondering how she was going to stand spending so much time with Viktor.

CHAPTER 2

By the time Serafina returned to the blacksmith shop, Alek had finished working on the sword for the day and had helped his father take the axle off the farmer's wagon. Since the time he was old enough to wield a hammer, Alek had worked in his father's shop. Although he was only a few years older than Serafina, he was nearly as tall as his six-foot-three-inch father. With his thick blond hair and easy smile lighting his handsome face, Alek attracted the attention of all the girls wherever he went.

"Can you take a break and go for a walk with me?" Serafina asked him.

He stood and brushed off his knees. "Let's go. I could use a breath of fresh air." After washing his hands and face in a bucket of water they kept by the door, he dried off with a piece of cloth and told his father, "I'll be back in a little while."

Taking Serafina's hand in his, Alek led her out the door to the road that fronted the blacksmith shop on its way to the center of town. They strolled past the narrow stone buildings that lined the streets, to the town square where serving girls lingered by the well, flirting with the older apprentices who stopped by. On the other side of the square stood the oak that had been there long before the oldest man in town was born.

"Remember when I made you climb this tree?" Alek asked as he and Serafina wandered into its shade.

Serafina nodded. "And I couldn't go higher than the first two branches. That's when I discovered that I was afraid of heights."

Alek laughed. "I had to help you down. You were shaking like a kitten in a wolf's den. But that wasn't the part I meant. That was the day I kissed you for the first time."

"I remember. I didn't know if I should kiss you back or run home and tell my mother," she said with a smile. Although Serafina's dark hair and deep blue eyes were pretty enough to turn heads, everyone said that she was most beautiful when she smiled. Alek made her smile more than anyone else.

"I'm glad you decided to kiss me. Who knows what would have happened if you'd told your mother. That reminds me—did you read the letter? Who sent it? Let me guess: someone is coming for a visit."

"Not quite," Serafina said. "My great-aunt Sylanna wants me to visit her."

"I didn't know you had a great-aunt Sylanna. I thought I'd met all your relatives."

"I didn't know about her, either, but it seems she wants to give me some sort of inheritance. What we can't understand is why she's giving it to me and not to Alina or Katya."

"What is she giving you?"

"She didn't say. All she said was that it was going to change my life. We think it's either money or a small business. I have to go to Mala Kapusta tomorrow. Father won't be back in time, so Mother has asked Viktor to take me."

"Viktor!" Alek said as if he had tasted something bad. "That man is a bully and a liar. Couldn't your mother find someone else? I would go if she'd let me."

"And set all the gossips' tongues wagging? Mother would never allow it. Besides, you need to finish that

14

sword for Sir Ganya. Didn't he say that he wants it as soon as possible? Don't worry. I should be gone only a few days. Mother thinks Great-Aunt Sylanna will invite us to stay overnight; then we'll be back the next day."

"I don't like it," Alek said, scowling. "You're going to spend an entire day with Viktor so you can see a relative you don't know. And this inheritance . . . What if it is a business and your great-aunt expects you to live in Mala Kapusta?"

"If she does, I suppose I'll have to consider it," Serafina said with a shrug. "But I won't make any decisions right away."

"But it is possible that you could move there."

"I suppose it's *possible*," Serafina replied.

Alek sighed and stopped walking. "Then there's something else for you to consider before you make any big decisions," he said, turning her so that she faced him. "I've wanted to ask you something for a while, but the time never seemed right. Now I guess I have to just come out and say it. I mean, if you're going to make life-changing decisions, I want you to take something important into account. I love you, Serafina Divis, and I have for a very long time. I know our parents think we're too young to get engaged, but I would like to give you this." Reaching into his pocket, Alek took out an ornate gold heart twice as big as his thumbnail. "It was my mother's, and her mother's before that. My mother used to wear it on a gold chain, but when she was dying she took it off and gave it to me, saying that it would remind me how much she loved me. I've been carrying it in my pocket ever since, but now I want you to have it to remind you how much I love you. Think of it as a preengagement token."

Serafina felt tears come to her eyes. She remembered his mother wearing the necklace, though Serafina didn't know that his mother had given the heart to him. Serafina also knew how much Alek missed his mother, who had died three years ago, and how precious this keepsake must be to him. Although she had long thought that she would marry Alek someday, they had never really talked about it. "Are you proposing to me, Alek?"

He gave her a nervous grin. "I'm telling you that I want to propose someday. It's early yet, but I want you to know just how serious I am."

"I would love to wear the heart, Alek," she said, gazing into his eyes. "I have a gold chain that would be perfect for it. And when we're old enough, I would love to marry you."

Serafina didn't know how nervous Alek was until he

breathed a sigh of relief and gathered her into his arms. "Thank goodness," he murmured into her hair. "I don't know what I would have done if you had turned me down!"

"Watch out!" shouted a man driving a wagon full of barrels. Two of the apprentices had gotten into a shoving match, and one had fallen into the street right in front of the wagon. The horse pulling the wagon shied to the side. One of the wheels popped off and rolled toward an elderly couple, just missing them. The wagon tipped and the barrels shifted their weight. Leaning precariously, the wagon pulled at the traces, making the horse rear and scream.

"Stay here!" Alek said, pushing Serafina to safety.

"Whoa, boy!" he said in a calming voice. When the horse's front hooves touched the ground again, Alek jumped to grab the reins. The horse's eyes were wide, his ears pinned back to his skull as he tried to jerk his head away, but Alek held tight, talking in a soothing way until the animal stopped trying to get free and stood, sides heaving and nostrils flaring.

Serafina held her breath as Alek stroked the horse's neck, but the animal was calmer now and did nothing more than paw the ground. Alek stood with the horse while the driver and the two apprentices put the wheel back on the wagon and returned the barrels to their places.

Serafina watched Alek, her eyes filled with pride. He was always jumping in to help others, even when no one else would. His big heart was one of the reasons she loved him so much. It was also one of the reasons she couldn't imagine her life without him. Although she had been uncertain about the trip to Mala Kapusta at first, knowing that he loved her so made Serafina feel as if she could handle anything.

CHAPTER 3

Serafina and Viktor left for Mala Kapusta early on market day. It would take many hours to reach the small town, which was just past the border in the kingdom of Vargas. Her mother and sisters were there to see her off, still talking about Serafina's inheritance and what she should do with it if it was indeed money. Although she couldn't wait to leave so she wouldn't have to hear any more of their suggestions, being alone with Viktor when the coach started rolling was worse.

They sat side by side in the confined space of a rented carriage. Viktor's nose whistled when he breathed and he picked his teeth with his pinky finger, flicking what he found onto the floor. The first time he did it, Serafina turned away in disgust and watched the town creep past as the coachman edged around stopped wagons and dawdling people. Then, suddenly, an old woman emptying a chamber pot out a second-story window startled the horses, and the coachmen had to climb down from his seat to calm them.

"Do you know how much of an inconvenience this is?" Viktor asked her as the coach began to move again. "I had to postpone an important meeting I had planned for today. I better get something out of this."

"You mean aside from my thanks?" asked Serafina.

"I mean some of whatever the old woman is giving you tonight. It costs a lot to support your sister, and I have other expenses as well."

"I don't know if she's giving me money."

Viktor shrugged. "Whatever it is, I want some. You're supposed to be smart. I'm sure you can figure something out."

"But—"

"No more talking," Viktor said, shutting his eyes. "I need my rest."

By the time they entered the countryside, Viktor was asleep with his mouth open and his head tilted back. He snored in raspy snorts and breathy grunts, his snoring as loud as the carriage wheels jouncing over the rutted road. Serafina couldn't help but think about what it would have been like if Alek had been there instead. They would have sat close together, looking out the same window, pointing out the things that caught their eye, sharing their thoughts and laughing when they saw something funny. Alek would have told her some of his bad jokes, and she would have laughed simply because he found them so amusing. When they grew tired of that, they would have talked about their plans for the future. After a while she probably would have dozed off holding one of Alek's strong, callused hands. Her head would have been pillowed against his shoulder and—

Serafina gasped when Viktor snorted and flung his arm wide in his sleep, hitting her with his hand. She edged as far from him as she could and sat bolt upright for a while after that. Although she'd doubted she'd be able to sleep sitting next to him, Serafina eventually dozed off, wondering how her sister could stand Viktor.

* * *

It was early evening when they finally reached Mala Kapusta. It was a medium-sized town that had been established at a well-traveled crossroad and spread into the forest on either side. Most of the houses were made of wood, with curved roofs and carvings decorating the lintels and eaves. Painted bright colors, the buildings contrasted with the greens of the surrounding forest. Although trees had been cut down within the town, the forest was still close enough to give one a sheltered feeling.

The carriage stopped in front of an inn with a swinging wooden sign that bore the picture of a bloody tooth and a rusty nail. The coachman opened the door and reached in to help Serafina, but Viktor pushed her back and climbed out first, saying to the man, "Collect our bags while I arrange for our supper."

Serafina glanced down the street, waiting for the coachman to retrieve their two overnight bags from the carriage. Taking a deep breath, she filled her lungs with the scent of the fir trees of the forest and the honeysuckle that grew in yellow and white profusion beside the inn.

"Stop staring like a simpleton and bring those bags inside, Serafina," Viktor said from the door of the inn. "I've told the innkeeper that we'll be having supper here. I turned him down when he asked if we wanted rooms. I think it's odd that your great-aunt wants us to come to her house so late at night, but then, wealthy people are often eccentric."

The innkeeper, a smiling, friendly-seeming man, nodded from where he waited behind Viktor. "That's very true," he said, although Serafina had the feeling that he would have agreed with anything Viktor said.

They ate their supper in silence. Viktor devoured all his portion of the pork pie, crusty herb bread, and soft cheese as if he were starving, then scraped the rest of Serafina's onto his own plate. She was about to protest but decided that it wasn't worth an argument.

Serafina jumped when Viktor slapped his tankard on the table. "Where is that serving girl?" he demanded, looking around. Spotting her in the far corner talking to another patron, he waved to catch her eye. When she didn't acknowledge him, he stuck two fingers in his mouth and whistled. The girl gave him a horrified look and started across the room.

"If Widow Zloto were here, she'd tell you that it's bad luck to whistle inside," said Serafina.

"Oh, really?" said Viktor. "This is how much I care about Widow Zloto and her superstitions!" He snapped his fingers inches from Serafina's face and smirked when she jerked away from him. Sticking his fingers in his mouth again, he whistled even louder.

"Please don't do that, sir," the serving girl said, bobbing a curtsy. "Don't you know it's bad luck to whistle inside a building?"

Viktor smiled at the girl and shook his head. "No, I didn't know that. In that case, I won't do it again!"

The innkeeper appeared behind the girl. Seeing Viktor's empty tankard, he gestured to it, saying, "Fill this for our guest, Mila." As the girl hurried off to fetch a pitcher, the innkeeper pulled another chair to the table and sat down. "So," the man said to Serafina, "your brother-in-law tells me that you've come to see your great-aunt."

Serafina glanced at Viktor, annoyed that he'd told the man her personal business.

"You may know the woman," said Viktor. "Her name is Sylanna."

The man looked puzzled. "I can't say that I'm familiar with the name, and I thought I knew everyone. Maybe she goes by another name here."

Serafina glanced out the window. It was already dark and she could see the first star in the sky. "Shouldn't we go soon?"

"Not yet," Viktor said as he watched the serving girl approach with a pitcher. "We have plenty of time."

"How far are we from a tavern called the Bialy Jelen?" Serafina asked the innkeeper.

"Not far," he said as the girl refilled Viktor's tankard. "Just turn left, then left again at the corner. The Bialy

24

Jelen is at the edge of the forest. If you're worried about the time, listen for the church bells. The last one rang at 8:30."

"We need to go, Viktor," Serafina said, reaching for her bag.

"He said it wasn't far. I'm going to finish this first," Viktor said, and took a long, noisy gulp of mead.

"Fine, then you can stay here and I'll find it myself. I'm not going to be late for something this important just because you want to drink."

"I'm coming!" Viktor grumbled, reluctantly setting the tankard back on the table. "But I've heard it's bad luck if you don't finish all of your drink!"

* * *

When they left the inn, the lights spilling from the cottage windows made it easy to see, but as the homes gave way to shops that were closed for the night, the street became darker and the shadows more ominous. The moon was just the smallest sliver in the sky, giving them little additional light. Serafina glanced at Viktor, who was walking in the middle of the street, turning his head from side to side as if he expected something to jump out at him. "Don't you think it's odd that the innkeeper didn't know Sylanna?" Serafina asked him. "This town isn't that big; I should think everyone would know everyone else."

Viktor began to hurry when a well-lit tavern at the end of the row of shops came into view. "She's probably an eccentric old woman who keeps to herself," he said. "Or maybe he knows her, but the townspeople don't like talking about one another to strangers."

They were passing the Bialy Jelen when Viktor peered ahead and came to a sudden stop. "This is the last building. I don't see any houses here. We must have turned the wrong way. We have to go back."

Serafina shook her head. "We turned left, like the innkeeper said. It has to be here somewhere. The letter said it was just past the tavern called the Bialy Jelen. Wait, there's a house set back from the road. I think I see a candle in a window."

"It's too dark . . . ," Viktor said, lingering near the tavern and the last pool of light. He was still there when Serafina left the road. "You probably made us come on the wrong day," he called after her. "It doesn't look as if anyone is expecting us. I doubt that's even a house."

"This is the right day," said Serafina. "And this is a house. See, there's a fence around it." It was lumpy and uneven, but it was white, so at least she could see it. Serafina had scarcely set her hand on the gate when it swung open with a loud creak.

"What was that?" Viktor demanded.

26

Serafina glanced back to see that he was still standing in the road.

"Just the gate," she told him, and turned toward the house. From what she could see, it was a small building with an overhanging roof, but it was set so close to the forest that the starlight didn't reach it and she couldn't make out any details.

Viktor had yet to approach the gate when Serafina knocked on the door. "Aunt Sylanna?" she called, stepping inside. "It's me, Serafina."

Sparkling light shimmered in the corner by the bed. It was so bright that Serafina had to close her eyes and rub them. When she opened them again, a single candle flickered on a table by the window. Aside from the fire in the tile stove in the corner, it was the only source of light in the one-room cottage, but it was enough to show her that no one else was there. *I must be imagining things*, Serafina thought.

Suddenly Viktor, who was still standing outside, shouted with surprise. Serafina turned to see why and saw that the gate had slammed shut on its own. She was about to call to her brother-in-law when a cat ran over the threshold.

"Chicken hut, chicken hut, take us away!" shouted a voice inside the cottage. Then the door to the cottage closed with a bang as the floor tilted beneath Serafina's feet. She staggered and fell to her hands and knees, sliding backward until she bumped into a chair. When the cottage began to rise, Serafina grabbed hold of a chair leg.

Serafina's stomach plummeted as the cottage rose, stopped with a lurch, and leveled off. She was struggling to her feet when the door slammed open. A mass of white objects flew into the cottage. The breeze created when they whipped past made the candle gutter and go out.

Serafina stepped into the middle of the cottage, hoping to get to the door. "Oof!" she cried when one last object flew through the opening and hit her in the stomach. Enough light was coming through the window now that she could make out the object's shape. Round and white, it fell to the floor and began to roll away. Curious, Serafina bent down and picked it up. She couldn't tell what it was until she brought it close to her face. Her breath caught in her throat when she realized that it was a skull.

"What are you looking at?" the skull asked her, its jaw moving in her hands.

For the first time in her life, Serafina fainted.

CHAPTER 4

Serafina woke with her head lolling from side to side on the hard wood floor. The cottage was swaying back and forth in a rhythmic way and felt as if it was moving forward. Bracing herself, Serafina sat up and looked around. The fire crackling in the stove and the meager amount of light coming through the windows allowed her to see vague outlines but little more. Hoping to find the candle, she stood and gingerly worked her way to a table in front of one of the windows. The candle was there, along with a flint to light it.

Serafina exhaled in relief when the wick caught. Holding the candle high, she peered into the dim corners of the cottage. It was a simple room with a narrow bed on one side and a tile-covered stove on the other.

Logs burned in the stove, snapping and crackling each time the cottage lurched. Water sloshed in a bucket in the corner but didn't quite spill over the edge. The table standing against a side wall and the two wooden chairs facing the table didn't budge, no matter how much the cottage moved. The only windows in the cottage were on either side of the door, and both held panes of wavy glass. Now that she could see more clearly, she noticed that what she had thought were tables under the windows were actually storage trunks.

Something stirred on the bed, startling Serafina. When she turned in that direction, two red eyes reflected the light of the candle. Her heart began to race as she remembered the skull, but when she heard a catlike *"Mrowr!"* she almost laughed with relief. A large black cat with a small patch of white on his chest was reclining on the bed, watching her.

"If only you could talk," Serafina told him. "I bet you could tell me what's going on."

The cat's eyes were still on her when he stood up and stretched. He was at least twice the size of the cats that begged for scraps at the kitchen door at home. When he jumped off the bed and started toward her, she wasn't sure if he was being friendly or aggressive. The cat strolled right past her, however, crossing the length of the room to hop up onto the table. Using one paw, he poked at something and began to purr so loudly that Serafina could hear him from where she stood.

Curious, Serafina walked toward the table, trying to see what interested the cat. It was a book, its leather cover scarred and discolored from age. The cat moved aside at Serafina's approach and turned to sit facing her. Placing the candle on the table, Serafina lifted the book's cover. The page inside was blank, but even as she reached to turn the page, letters began to form on the pure white sheet.

> Welcome! You are the new Baba Yaga and the mistress of this house. As Baba Yaga, you will have certain duties to perform. Your first duty is to take care of this house and the cat. Treat them well and they will treat you well. Your other duties will become clear to you in time.

Serafina read the words over again. When it didn't look as if any more writing was going to appear, she turned the page and waited. Nothing happened. She turned the next page and the next, until she reached the back of the book. Every page but the first one was blank.

Her mind was racing when she returned to the front of the book. Was this some kind of joke? If it was, it wasn't the least bit funny. She looked around the cottage, hoping to see the person behind it all, but she was still alone with a cat and a book that didn't make any sense.

Serafina turned back to the book, frowning. Baba Yaga? Everyone knew that was just a character in a fairy tale and not a real person. Was she supposed to stay in this house? And what were these mysterious duties? Was this her inheritance? If it was, she didn't want it! She would go home and forget all about Great-Aunt Sylanna and her promises. Nothing was going to keep her here now! She doubted that Viktor was still waiting for her, but she really didn't need him. She'd go back to the inn, and if Viktor wasn't there, she'd have the innkeeper find her a coach to hire. Her mother would gladly pay for it once she returned home safe and sound.

Serafina glanced at the closest window. It was still night, but she didn't care. She was determined to go home immediately. Clutching the candle in her hand, she strode across the swaying floor to the door, but when she tried to wrench it open, it refused to budge. She tried again, but the door was firmly closed, as if it were one piece with the wall. Squeezing her hand into a fist, she banged on the door. Aside from hurting her hand, nothing happened.

Serafina turned to the window next, but it was sealed shut and apparently not meant to open. She could break the glass if she had to, although— A soft sound behind her made her whirl around. It was just the cat, jumping back onto the bed. The first hint of despair touched Serafina's heart, but she wasn't ready to give in. There must be something she could use here, something that would help her get out.

Holding the candle high, Serafina bent down and opened the wax-splattered trunk lid. When the light fell on fabric, she reached in and pulled out a gown. There was another gown under the first, and below that were more gowns and a shawl so soft that she couldn't resist setting it to the side. On closer inspection, she discovered that the gowns were all different sizes and styles. Some of the gowns would surely fit her, but others would be much too large or far too long. There were undergarments there as well as clothes to wear to bed. It was a large trunk, but Serafina was amazed by how much it held.

After returning everything to the trunk except the shawl, she closed the lid and crossed to the other trunk. She opened it expecting to find something as innocuous as clothing, but she gasped and nearly dropped the candle when she saw what was inside. The second trunk was just as large as the first and was filled with human bones. Leg bones, arm bones, and finger bones were heaped inside, with skulls piled high on top.

"Shut the lid!" ordered one of the skulls. "Can't you see we're trying to sleep?"

Serafina gasped. A skull really was talking to her! She thought she'd imagined it before.

"That's a good one, Boris!" said another skull. "As if we ever sleep! What are we going to do, close our eyes?"

"If you slept, I bet you'd snore, Krany. From the size of your nose hole, you must have had an enormous honker!"

"I bet my brain was bigger, too, Yure! Certainly bigger than yours."

"Why, I oughtta—"

Serafina took a deep breath to calm her racing heart. Given a choice, she would never have talked to skulls, but there wasn't anyone else there. "Pardon me, but could you please answer a few questions?"

"Who? Us? Why should we?" said the skull named Boris.

"To help a stranger in need?" she said as if she wasn't sure why herself.

"Ha!" said Krany. "No one has ever helped us!"

"What sort of questions?" Yure asked.

"How can I get out of here?" said Serafina. "Why am I here? Where's my great-aunt Sylanna?"

"Oh! Oh!" squealed Krany. "Let me answer one! The answer to your first question is, you can't get out of the cottage until the chicken gets to where it's going. Do I win? Do I get a prize now?"

"I want one, too!" said Yure.

"What chicken?" asked Serafina, looking around the room.

"Ask me a *good* question," Yure cried. "Make it a hard one. I can handle it."

"Fine. How are you able to talk? Is this cottage really moving? If it is, how is that possible? Why are you in this trunk? How did those words appear in that book? Did the cat really show me the book on purpose? Why am I talking to a bunch of skulls? Am I going crazy?"

"Uh," Yure began. "The answer is . . . no! You're not going crazy! There! I did it! Now you owe me a prize, too."

Serafina sighed. "Just tell me where I can find my great-aunt Sylanna. She can explain it all."

"Si-who-a?" asked Yure. "I've never heard of her." The skull shifted in the trunk until he was facing down.

"Anyone down there named Si something or other?" he called.

"Anyone down there an aunt?" shouted Krany. "Because *that* would be a real surprise."

Muted voices rumbled in the trunk, then one of the skulls toward the bottom of the pile called back, "No aunts down here."

"No one named Sigh, either," shouted another skull.

Serafina rocked back on her heels. "Never mind. If you don't want to help me, you could just say so."

"What's my prize?" Krany asked.

"Your prize is . . . you can go back to sleep," Serafina said, shutting the lid of the trunk.

"Well, that's a lousy prize," grumbled the muffled voice of a skull.

"It's better than nothing," another skull replied.

Serafina stepped away from the trunk. She was afraid, she was worried, but most of all, she was confused. A chicken she couldn't see, a moving cottage, a book that wrote its own words, and a trunk full of talking skulls couldn't be real, could they? Unless . . . Was it possible that this was magic? Growing up, Serafina had heard rumors that magic existed, but most of the people she knew scoffed at anyone who claimed that it was real. She had heard of Baba Yaga, of course, but her parents had told her that the witch was just part of a fairy tale and that only the weak-minded or deluded believed in her. Even the superstitious Nesha Zloto claimed that Baba Yaga couldn't possibly exist.

Moving closer to the window, Serafina glanced out and her hand flew to her mouth. She was in the forest now, and the tops of the trees seemed to be streaming past. But the way the floor was shifting beneath her feet, it had to be the cottage that was moving, not the forest, and she had to be up high. Serafina hated heights. Even if the door was open, she wouldn't go near it now.

When an owl swooped in front of the window, Serafina retreated to the middle of the room. There wasn't a thing she could do in the dark inside a moving building. Who knew where she was or how high above the ground she might be?

Suddenly it was all so overwhelming that Serafina couldn't handle any more. Only this morning she had left her family to spend the day driving with Viktor. Who knew what she'd find when the cottage finally stopped moving?

Taking the shawl she'd found in the trunk, she shuffled to the bed. Tears trickled from the corners of her eyes while she draped the shawl around herself and lay down. She pulled a golden chain from inside her bodice and wrapped her fingers around the heart Alek had given her, and pressed it to her lips. If only Alek were here with her, he would know what to do!

Serafina had never felt so desolate, so lost, so *alone* before. She had always had her family or Alek to turn to, and now there was no one but a weird, oversized cat and some squabbling skulls. From the way the cottage was still moving, she doubted that she was anywhere near Mala Kapusta. For all she knew, the cottage might have carried her to another kingdom.

She moved her feet and nudged the cat with her heel. He growled, so she moved her foot away again. "Sorry," she said, her breath catching in her throat with a sob.

Serafina was on the verge of sleep when a soft voice replied, "That's quite all right." She was sure she was dreaming already.

Chapter 5

The scents of candle wax and cat and the mustiness of an old house reminded Serafina where she was before she even opened her eyes, but she knew right away that something had changed. She couldn't think of what it might be, except— Her eyes flew open when she realized that the cottage was no longer moving. She sat up and tossed back the covers, which landed on the cat. The animal grumbled but didn't move, even after Serafina wiggled off the bed. Without a backward glance, Serafina stumbled toward the door and threw it open. Sunshine and fresh air flooded into the cottage.

The trees that surrounded the cottage looked older and taller than the forest that enclosed the town of Mala Kapusta. The air outside smelled of damp earth and growing things, but there wasn't even a hint of wood smoke or any of the other odors that betrayed the presence of a town or village. She was surprised to see that there was a fence around the cottage, just as there had been the night before. What she hadn't realized then was that the fence was made of bones—leg bones, arm bones, and finger bones, with a skull topping every other post. Serafina thought that they were probably the very same bones and skulls that she'd found in the trunk. It occurred to her that Sylanna might have had her come at night so she wouldn't see the fence. "I probably wouldn't have come into the yard if I'd seen that," she murmured to herself.

Serafina had no idea where she was or how to get home, but now that she could get the door open, she wasn't about to stay in Sylanna's cottage a moment longer. This wasn't an inheritance. It was a kidnapping! Viktor had said that he wanted part of whatever Si-who-a gave her. Serafina would have been delighted to give him the whole thing!

Although Serafina didn't want to touch the fence, she couldn't think of any way to avoid it, unless . . . She had the bag she'd brought with her, but it held only a single change of clothes and a hairbrush—nothing that she could use for what she had in mind. Taking one last look at the cottage, she spotted the shawl she'd left draped across the foot of the bed. "That will do," she muttered, and stepped back into the room to fetch it. After closing the cottage door behind her, she hurried toward the gate while wrapping the shawl around her hand.

She had just reached for the finger-bone latch when the skull on the gatepost cried out, "Where do you think you're going?" Its jaw made a creaking sound when it moved, like the bones of an old man getting out of bed. Serafina thought it might be Boris, the skull who had first spoken to her the night before.

"As far away from here as I can get!" Serafina said, tugging on the gate. "Now open up!"

"She's trying to leave!" said the one she thought might be Yure.

"We can see that," the skull called Krany cried. "Someone has to stop her!"

The skulls all began to shout at her at once. Serafina let go of the latch and took a step back; the racket stopped immediately. It started up again as soon as she put her hand back on the finger bone. Serafina shook her head. "You can't keep me here with a little noise," she said, and wrenched the gate with all her might until it popped open. The shouting turned to wails of anguish.

"Yow!" shouted Boris over the noise his friends were making. "Did you see what she did? She would have broken my finger bone if I hadn't let go!"

Serafina hurried away from the cottage. "I'm sorry!" she shouted over her shoulder. "But you wouldn't let me out!"

"Don't go!" cried Boris. "You don't know what you're doing!"

"Oh yes, I do," Serafina announced. "I'm going home!"

The cottage had settled at the edge of an old animal trail, which was enough of a path for Serafina. At first the ground was too uneven for her to go very fast, but after a while it became smoother; she was nearly running when the path intersected a road. She had no idea where she was or which way to go. After a moment of indecision, she turned right and started running as fast as she could. Serafina wanted to get as far from the cottage as possible, but when her lungs felt as if they were burning and her legs hurt, she was forced to slow down to a steady walk. She was sure that she'd reach a village sooner or later, and when she did, she would find out where she was and what it would take to get home.

Serafina had stopped to rest for a moment when she saw a figure approaching from the opposite direction. At first she was worried about meeting a stranger in the middle of the woods and thought about hiding until he passed, but she hesitated long enough to see that he was an old man, bent nearly double under the weight of a bundle of sticks.

The old man looked puzzled when he drew close enough to get a good look at her. "What are you doing in these woods all by yourself, young miss?" he asked.

Serafina was relieved that she might have found the sympathetic ear of someone who could help her. She was about to tell him everything that had happened to her, but when she opened her mouth to speak, the words she wanted to say wouldn't come out. Instead she said in an unfamiliar voice, "I'm running away from a house that moves on its own, skulls that talk, and a future that I find frightening but cannot escape. I must go back to the house to get the answers that I need."

When her mouth finally closed, Serafina stood frozen in place, too stunned to move. She hadn't even thought the words before she'd said them, and when she was talking, she'd had no control over her voice or her body. It was as if she was outside of herself, listening to someone else, and the words just happened to come from her. She had been frightened when the cottage moved, but now she felt terrified!

Serafina scarcely noticed when the old man gave her

an odd look and hurried on his way. As he disappeared down the road, she thought about what she had said. Was it true? Did she have to go back to find out what was going on? But what if she just went home? Then none of it really mattered, did it? She didn't want to have anything to do with the house or the skulls or her great-aunt Sylanna, whoever she was.

Serafina shook her head and started walking again, but she'd taken only a few steps when she noticed that her feet hurt and her dress felt tight across her chest. Glancing down, she saw that the fabric of her bodice was pulled taut, and she wasn't able to take a really deep breath. She tried wiggling her toes, but her shoes had suddenly become painfully small. What was going on? Had something in the cottage made her grow overnight? But then why hadn't she noticed it sooner? She was running before, but now she doubted she could even walk very far with her shoes on.

Serafina had taken off one of her shoes to examine it when she heard the sound of laughter. She raised her head and saw a young man and a young woman walking beside a cart piled high with their belongings. As they drew closer, she saw that a baby was nestled among the baggage, sound asleep.

"Hello!" the young man said when he saw her.

The young woman gave her a warm smile. "We're on our way to Mala Las. Do you happen to know how far it is from here?"

Serafina had no idea where she was or how far it was to anywhere. She began to shake her head, but once again she lost control of her body. Her arm raised itself and she pointed down the road. Words came pouring out of her mouth. "Mala Las is twelve miles in that direction if you stay on this road. However, if you walk six miles you will find another road leading off to your right. Turn onto that road; walk two and a half miles and you will reach Mala Las in time to eat supper with your uncle Rybar."

The young man frowned. "How did you know about my wife's uncle? We didn't mention that we were going to see him."

"Did you notice her eyes, Petruso?" the young woman asked him. "They got all funny when she started to talk."

Serafina dropped her arm the moment she had control of her body again. When she tried to take a breath, she couldn't draw air into her lungs and she gasped instead. Her gown was so tight that she couldn't breathe. If she could have spoken, she would have asked the couple for help, but they hurried off so quickly that she didn't have the chance. Her fingers fumbled as she tried to loosen the strings on her bodice; she was seeing spots in front of her eyes before she could get the strings undone. When she was finally able to breathe again, she took in great gulps of air and sat down until she could stop shaking. Her feet were throbbing when she took off her shoes. Given how tight they had been on her feet, she doubted very much that she'd be able to get them back on.

Serafina stared at the ground without really seeing it. Twice now someone had spoken to her, and when she had been about to reply, she had lost control and told them things she didn't know she'd known. Each time she had grown as well. Was she going to lose herself every time she talked to someone or grow every time she answered a question? What exactly had happened to her in that cottage? She hadn't had anything to eat or drink, so maybe it was something in the air. If only she knew what had happened, she might be able to do something about it.

Suddenly, returning home didn't seem like such a good idea. Something had happened in that cottage, and it looked as if she wasn't going to be able to leave it behind. She had to return to the cottage to get some answers. Although she dreaded the thought of going back there, she didn't seem to have any choice.

Barefoot and limping, Serafina turned around and headed back the way she had come, hoping she would find the path to the cottage before too long. Just how far had she gone, anyway?

CHAPTER 6

Serafina's feet hurt. "Ow!" she cried, stepping on yet another stone. She wished she could put her shoes on again, but her feet had grown too big. She was examining the damage to her foot when she heard a faint trill of laughter. Turning toward the sound, she saw butterflies flitting around a patch of dandelions. Or maybe they were hummingbirds. She squinted, certain that her eyes were playing tricks on her, because they could just as easily be dragonflies, but not really. Her mouth dropped when she realized that they had the faces and tiny bodies of humans and the gossamer wings of some ethereal creature. "What on earth?" she said, taking a step closer.

One of the little creatures saw her watching them. It

shouted at its friends, and they all turned and fled deeper into the forest.

Serafina shook her head. Those creatures couldn't possibly be fairies, could they? Fairies weren't real! She'd heard stories about fairies, of course, but that's all they were—stories. Her mother had told her so when she was little, and her sisters had laughed at her for even hinting that she might believe in them. But she could swear that she had just seen some. Either she was losing her mind or all those people who had told her that things like magic and fairies weren't real were actually wrong. If only she could talk to Alek about it. If she told her family, they wouldn't believe her, but Alek would be interested. He was always reading books about things other people thought were outlandish, like werewolves and sea monsters. Wait until she told him that she had seen fairies!

After one last glance at the forest where the fairies had disappeared, Serafina started walking again, wincing with each step.

* * *

"There she is! I told you she'd come back," cried Krany as Serafina staggered up the path.

"No, you didn't!" said Yure. "You said she shot out of here faster than a pack of lice fleeing an ogre's crunchy underpants on wash day and we'd never see her again."

"But then I said—"

"Never mind! She's here now, so I won!" Boris told them. "I said she'd be back before dark."

Serafina's feet were cut and bleeding. She was tired and sore and in no mood to deal with the skulls. Gritting her teeth, she reached for the latch, but before she could touch it, the gate swung open with a loud creak. Serafina hesitated. It occurred to her that she could still go home. Her family would be overjoyed to see her and would help her in whatever way they could. But if she went home, she'd disrupt her family with her bizarre problems, and that was something she didn't want to do.

Serafina had always thought of Alina as the sister who got into messes, like the day she and her friends stole walnuts from a neighbor's tree. The rest of her friends escaped, but Alina was caught because she had filled her pockets so full that she couldn't fit through the gap in the fence. Katya, the oldest, had been the obedient daughter, who did what she thought her parents wanted her to do, including marrying Viktor. Serafina, however, had always considered herself the smart daughter, who did what she thought was right. And now she had to find out for herself what was really going on.

Straightening her shoulders, Serafina stepped through the gate. The answer to what was happening to her might well be waiting for her in this cottage.

She ignored the skulls' snickering and raised her hand to the latch, but the door swung open just as the gate had.

"So you're back!" said a voice.

Serafina looked around. The only one there was the cat, still on the bed where she'd left him that morning. He was sitting up now with his tail wrapped around his legs, his green eyes fixed on her. The night before, she'd thought she had dreamed that the cat had spoken to her, but maybe it hadn't been a dream at all. Maybe the cat really had been talking. So many other unexplainable things had happened that she was beginning to think anything was possible. If skulls and a cat could talk to her, what was next, the teacups?

"I was sure you'd return sooner or later. New Baba Yagas always do," the cat continued. "Their lives are ruined if they don't."

"You mean Baba Yagas are real?" Serafina said, still not quite believing that she was conversing with a cat.

"Of course they're real," said the cat. "There have been Baba Yagas for hundreds of years."

"Some of the skulls didn't think I'd be back."

"The ignorant ones were saying that you were gone for good," said the cat. "They forget that a new Baba Yaga has to learn what it means to *be* Baba Yaga, and this is the best place to do that. The rest of the skulls were placing bets on when you'd show up again. You were faster than most, but then you're probably one of the smarter ones."

"Have there been a lot of Baba Yagas before me?" asked Serafina.

"More than I can count, but I'm a cat and not very good at counting."

"If I'm the new Baba Yaga, what happened to the old one? It wasn't my great-aunt Sylanna, was it?"

The cat twitched his tail. "The only name I know is 'Baba Yaga.' The last one left when you showed up. Didn't you see those sparkly lights when you walked in? That was the fairy whisking her away. Baba Yaga was dying, and the fairy Summer Rose had promised to take her to a beautiful place to live out her last days once she had a replacement. Although Baba Yaga wanted to stay to teach you what you needed to know, she was too sick by the time you got here. She asked me to tell the cottage to go as soon as you were inside so you couldn't leave and so you would have time to learn about being Baba Yaga. I thought she was a nice enough person, although she didn't like cats as much as some of the Baba Yagas before her did."

"You talk as if you've met the other Baba Yagas."

"That might be because I have," he said, sounding sarcastic. "My original owner was the nasty witch who started it all. She was a crazy, evil lowlife, but she knew her curses. I was just past kittenhood when she cursed me to live as long as Baba Yaga, and since there's been one person after another holding the title, I'm still here."

"Do you have a name?"

The cat made a funny little sound in his throat, which Serafina thought meant he was laughing. "I have lots of names! Octavius, Gwawl, Evrawg, Drefan. The last Baba Yaga to give me a name called me Viktor."

"I can't call you that! One of my brothers-in-law is named Viktor, and I don't like him one bit. I think I'll call you Maks."

"My uncle's name was Maksimillian."

"Then it's perfect!"

"Huh," grunted the cat.

"Why have there been so many Baba Yagas?"

Maks gave her a disgusted look. "That's enough questions; answering questions isn't *my* job."

"There's no one else I can ask," said Serafina, but the cat turned away and began to lick the base of his tail.

Serafina sighed, but the bodice of her dress was still so tight that deep breaths were uncomfortable. "At least I can do something about that," she murmured to herself, and turned to the trunk at the right of the doorway.

There were a lot of gowns in the trunk, but only a few fit her. When she'd selected the one she wanted, she started to take off her old clothes—until she noticed that the cat was watching her. "He's just a cat," she told herself, but she found his gaze disconcerting, so she went into the corner of the cottage farthest from the bed and turned her back to the cat before slipping off her under-shift.

Serafina was folding her old clothes when she noticed a bowl of slightly withered apples on the table. She was hungry enough not to care how an apple looked as long as it wasn't rotten, so she plucked one from the bowl and bit into it. When her glance fell on the book lying open on the table, she sat down and turned to the message that had greeted her as Baba Yaga. The rest of the pages were still blank.

"I was hoping this book would tell me what was going on," she said to herself.

Words began to appear on the blank sheet of parchment.

As the new Baba Yaga, you will answer
one question and only one for each person
who asks.

"What happens if I want to answer more than one?" she asked the book, but nothing else appeared on the page.

What good was a book that answered only some of her questions and only some of the time? Serafina slammed the book shut and shoved it away from her. "I don't want to be Baba Yaga!" she cried. "I want to go home!"

This wasn't fair! She was supposed to answer other people's questions while hers went unanswered? Suddenly it occurred to Seraphina that if she could answer their questions, she might be able to answer her own. "What is happening to me?" she said out loud, and waited. But she didn't lose control, or spout an answer, or feel any different.

"You can't answer your own questions," said Maks. "And you can't tell people what to ask you."

Serafina turned toward the cat. "If you know so much, why don't you just tell me what's going on and save us both a lot of—"

"Hello!" an old woman's voice called from outside the cottage.

Serafina hurried to the door. Maybe her great-aunt hadn't been that sick after all. Maybe Sylanna had come to tell her what to do. Peeking out the door, Serafina saw an old woman wearing a faded green shawl standing by the gate, one hand resting on a knobbed cane as she tried to lift the latch with the other. The old woman looked up as Serafina opened the door wider.

"Good," the woman said, giving Serafina a weary smile. "Someone is here. I've come to ask Baba Yaga my question."

Serafina couldn't help but feel disappointed that the woman wasn't Sylanna. Not sure what to do, she glanced back into the cottage. The cat was curled up again with his eyes closed. "You're no help," she muttered.

Her mind was racing as she faced the old woman. It wouldn't do Serafina any good to deny that she was Baba Yaga, not if she was going to have to answer questions whether she wanted to or not. It was even possible that by helping others, she might be able to help herself. Maybe by answering the questions, the answers she needed would present themselves somehow. Or maybe she had to answer a certain number of questions before she could go back to being her old self. She'd do anything that might help her return home. She just hoped it wouldn't take too long.

"Come in and sit down," she told the woman. "We can talk inside."

The old woman shuffled into the cottage, and Serafina showed her to the table. As her visitor sat down, Serafina moved to the other chair so she could sit facing the woman. "How can I help you?" she asked.

Her visitor looked surprised. "I won't ask if you're Baba Yaga and waste my question in such a foolish way. You didn't look like this when I saw you before, but I've heard rumors that your appearance often changes. Ah well, that's neither here nor there. For years I've been thinking about what question I would ask you. My age and poor health finally helped me decide. Before I forget, here's a loaf of fresh-baked bread to thank you for seeing me."

Serafina had noticed the bread's aroma the moment the old woman entered the cottage, but she thought the smell had just lingered on her visitor's clothes. When the woman pulled a string bag out from under her shawl and removed a loaf of crusty brown bread, Serafina's mouth began to water. Suddenly she was ravenous, and she would have eaten the bread then if her visitor hadn't been looking at her so expectantly. "What is your question?" she asked the woman, unable to take her eyes off the loaf.

"You've probably answered this question many times

before, but I need to know—what is going to happen to me when I die?"

Serafina had no idea how to answer, but her mouth opened of its own volition and she said, "You are a good woman and have shown others great kindness your entire life. You will die peacefully in your sleep this very month, and when you do, angels will come to escort you to heaven."

The old woman seemed satisfied with the answer, but Serafina must have looked distressed because her visitor leaned forward to pat her hand, saying, "Don't fret about me, my dear. Your answer was so much better than I expected. I was worried that I'd have to endure a long illness and upset my family with my suffering. Now I know that I should get my affairs in order and I don't have to worry that I will die in pain. Thank you, my dear. You've helped me more than you can know." There were tears in the old woman's eyes when she shuffled from the cottage, but Serafina noticed that a gentle smile curved her lips.

When Serafina stood to close the door, her dress felt uncomfortably tight again and her hem was inches above her ankles. "I need a mirror," she murmured, and let her gaze travel around the room.

In the far corner just past the bed stood a cupboard

so old that the wood was almost black. When Serafina opened the door, she was surprised to find that the cupboard was stocked with food and other essentials. One shelf held cups, plates, some old worn pots, and a handful of silverware. Another held a small sack of sugar, a larger sack of flour, a crust of stale bread, and a bag of potatoes that smelled as if they'd just been dug out of the earth. There were other food items on the next shelf, but it was a glimmer of light reflecting off something shiny that caught her eye. It was a small mirror, half-wrapped in a soft cloth. When she picked it up, she expected the mirror to be as old and serviceable as everything else in the cottage. Instead the frame was gold encrusted with finely wrought flowers made from amethysts and sapphires.

Normally Serafina might have enjoyed examining the craftsmanship of the frame, but the moment she caught sight of her reflection she couldn't look at anything else. She'd had the face and body of a girl when she came to get her inheritance, but now her cheeks were thinner and her hair was more lustrous. Glancing down, she saw that her body was as curvy and well-rounded as her older sisters'.

Serafina's heart pounded in her chest and she began to breathe too fast. Although she looked older, her mind was still the same as it had been before. What was happening to her?

Serafina was fighting off increasing panic when another voice called "Hello!" from outside the gate.

CHAPTER 7

Serafina missed Alek and her family fiercely and thought about them often. It had been more than two weeks since she'd seen them, and although she had started writing to her parents and sisters more than once to tell them that she was alive and well, she never got beyond the first few sentences. She wanted to tell them that she'd be home soon, but she had no idea how long she'd be gone. And how could she tell them about what had happened to her, when a fairy's magic had caused it and they didn't believe in either fairies or magic? She couldn't even tell them about her day-to-day life when that was so beyond anything they could understand.

She had also tried writing to Alek. He was more

likely to believe what had happened to her, and there was so much she wanted to tell him. The problem was that she was sure he would want to rescue her, but how could he rescue her from a curse that would follow her everywhere? Although she yearned to see him, she didn't want to entangle him in the mess that her life had become. Serafina had thrown out every letter to him that she'd started.

Fortunately for her, she was beginning to get used to her unusual life. She no longer hurried to look in the mirror after she answered each question, as she had for the first two weeks. There was no point; she knew that she looked like a mature woman now and she didn't want to see herself age. It helped that she had stopped growing after a few days and no longer had to look for new clothes in the trunk. It also helped that she knew what to expect. People came to her throughout the day, asking her questions about themselves or the ones they loved. Others came to her at night, stealing through the dark so that neither friends nor family would know of their visit. All of them brought her gifts to pay for her answers. Her larder was well stocked now, and on the rare occasion she thought of something she needed, all she had to do was mention it to one visitor and another would bring it.

After her first visitors, Serafina had decided on some

rules. She would invite guests into her cottage if they were polite. Only one person was allowed to come in at a time. She would set aside the normal rules of hospitality and offer her guests a drink or something to eat only if she wanted to. Both she and the guest would sit down before she asked for their question. And finally, she would not discuss one guest with another.

Even when Serafina didn't have visitors, her days were full. She took the responsibility of caring for the cat and house seriously, feeding the cat before she ate her own meals, cleaning the woodstove, restocking the basket beside it with logs, sweeping and dusting the cottage, and oiling the gate when it squeaked. Part of her hoped that by doing her best to fulfill her duties as Baba Yaga, she might be able to go home sooner. Another part of her enjoyed the responsibility of having her own home and making her own decisions. She might have been lonely if it weren't for the company of the cat and the skulls. Although the cat remained aloof at times, the skulls grew friendlier the longer she was there.

One morning Serafina was collecting berries from a thicket near the cottage when she felt as if someone was watching her. She turned around but didn't see anyone. Then suddenly there was a flash of brilliant blue, a whisper of pale pink, and a flicker of lilac. Serafina blinked, and when she opened her eyes, she was surrounded by a group of curious fairies. Not wanting to startle them, she held her breath as they drew close enough to touch. They hovered, just inches away, examining her as if she were a new species of flower. A hint of a breeze rustled the leaves, a tree branch creaked, and the fairies flew off in a whirl of color.

"I wonder if I passed the inspection," Serafina murmured as she returned to the berry patch.

* * *

Later that same day she was setting a jug of cider on a shelf when she decided that it was time to take a look at a few items in the cupboard a little more closely. Although she'd already searched through the cupboard more than once, she hadn't examined every single jar and bottle. There was one in particular that was worrying her. It was a black jar with a white skull painted on it. Lettering that was almost too small to read ran across the bottom. "What is this?" she asked, holding up the jar so Maks could see it. "Is it poison?"

The cat stopped licking his side long enough to glance her way. "I haven't seen that jar in years. That's skull polish. It cleans the skulls and makes them show up better in the dark."

Serafina squinted at the lettering. "'For best results, use once a month.'" She pried open the waxy lid and peered inside. "It's almost full."

"The skulls don't like being polished. A couple of the Baba Yagas tried to use it, but never more than once."

Serafina shook her head. "Like it or not, if those skulls are supposed to get polished, I'm going to do it. These should work," she said, taking some rags from the cupboard. "Do I have to leave the polish on for a minute or two, or should I wipe it off right away?"

"I don't know," said Maks. "That's never been an issue."

The cat followed Serafina out the door, lying down in a patch of sunlight to watch her. "Good luck!" he called as she approached Boris.

"What does he mean by that?" the skull asked Serafina. "Are you going somewhere?"

"Just to see you. I have a treat for you today. I'm going to polish you until you gleam." Tucking the jar lid in her pocket, she used a rag to scoop out a dab of polish and reached toward Boris.

"You're not getting that glop on me!" the skull declared. Rocking from side to side on his post, he turned his face away.

"That's fine. I'll start with the back of your head,"

Serafina said, and slapped him with the rag. "Then you don't have to see it."

"No!" cried Boris. "Don't touch me!"

"I already have," she said, rubbing the polish on his smooth surface.

"Ha-ha! Boris's getting polished!" chortled Yure.

"Be quiet, you brainless bonehead!" Boris shouted.

Serafina put another dollop of polish on Boris. "Don't worry," she told him. "I'll polish Yure next."

"Nooo!" Yure wailed. "Not me!"

"This is horrible!" Boris cried. "This is torture!"

"Oh, my. Look at that!" Serafina said, wiping off some of the polish.

"What is it? Is something wrong?" asked Boris.

"Nothing's wrong," Serafina told him. "It's just that you were looking a little dingy, but now, well . . . I've never seen such a brilliant white before. You really look quite handsome, Boris."

"This is an outrage!" declared Boris. "I told you I didn't . . . Did you say *brilliant*?"

"It almost hurts my eyes to look at you," said Serafina. "I can only imagine what you'll look like in the dark. Of course, you'd look even better if I could polish your front, too."

"Well," said Boris, "since you've started, you might

as well finish. Just be careful around my eye sockets. They're my best feature."

"He's letting you do it?" said Krany. His mouth opened so wide in disbelief that his bottom jaw dropped off. "Unh!" he groaned, tilting himself so he could see where his jawbone had landed in the grass.

Glancing at the incredulous skull, Serafina said, "I'll pick that up as soon as I finish with Boris."

"I knew something bad would happen if you polished us," cried Yure. "My grandfather always said, 'Never let a woman with a polishing cloth come near your naked skull.'"

"He did not say that," said Boris, angling himself so Serafina could get all the right spots. "He wouldn't have said anything like that unless he was bald, and you told me that all the men in your family had lots of hair."

"Well, he would have said it if he'd thought of it! Look at poor Krany. He must be really suffering."

Krany nodded and tried to talk. "Hunh hunh hunh hunh."

"Maybe I should help him now," said Serafina, stepping back from Boris.

Boris tilted himself to glance at her. "No! Don't stop! You're almost finished. I'm sure Krany's fine. Don't believe a word he says."

"I don't think he's said any actual words," Serafina told Boris as she began to apply more polish.

"Brilliant white, huh?" said Boris. "Just think, all those years I didn't want that stuff near me."

"And you called *me* a fool," Yure grumbled. "Don't forget," he told Serafina. "I'm next!"

By the time Serafina finished polishing the skulls, the sun was setting. She went inside to feed Maks and make her supper. When she was cleaning up afterward, she opened the door to let the cat out and overheard the skulls talking.

"She's not half-bad, you know, for a slip of a girl who has no idea what she's doing," said Krany.

"Are you kidding? She polished Boris! No one's ever done that before!"

"She polished all of us. You should see your face, Yure! It glows in the dark!"

"We all glow in the dark, Krany. Yourself included! I think it's kind of creepy."

"I like her," Boris announced. "She's taken to the job better than most, even though she didn't want it. I just hope she's doing as well in a few years."

"Years?" Serafina murmured, a cold knot forming in her stomach.

* * *

The next morning, Serafina sat at the table nursing a cup of cider while thinking about the people she'd met. In the beginning, she had dreaded answering questions, afraid of what she might say. The first time a man asked if his wife was trustworthy, he had stormed off in an awful temper when Serafina told him the truth. Another time a woman asked if she would ever have children and wept when she heard that she would die childless. Serafina soon learned that such moments were offset by the joyful news that she gave out, like the future birth of a much-wanted son to a kind couple or the knowledge that a loved one would overcome an illness and live a long and happy life. It frustrated her when people asked frivolous questions, such as the woman who wanted to know if she was a better cook than her mother-in-law or the man who asked which horse he should bet on in the next holiday's race, but she soon decided that it was their question to waste. Sometimes she wished that she could tell them to change their question, but nothing seemed to affect what they asked or what answers she gave.

Serafina yelped when Maks jumped onto her lap with his claws out. "Ow!" she exclaimed as there came a knock on the door. She glanced up when she heard another soft knock. "You didn't have to do that," she told the cat as she got to her feet.

"Yes, I did," Maks replied, examining his claws as he flexed them. "You looked like you were daydreaming and didn't notice when your next guest started knocking."

Serafina was surprised when she opened the door and found a girl no older than twelve standing with her hand raised, ready to knock again. The girl was the closest to Serafina's own real age of anyone who had come to visit her, and just seeing her was enough to remind Serafina of everything she had lost.

"I came to ask you my question. I brought you some flowers. See!" the girl said, holding out a bouquet of blossoms picked from a meadow. "I know we're supposed to bring something, but this is all I could think of."

Serafina gave herself a mental shake as if waking from a dream. "The flowers are fine, but you do realize that you can ask me only one question your entire life, don't you? Are you sure you want to ask me your question now?"

The girl nodded and shook the flowers at Serafina. "It's a very important question. It's about my mother. She's sick, you see, and—"

Serafina held up her hand. "Wait until you've come inside. I prefer to answer important questions while sitting down."

The girl followed Serafina into the cottage and took a seat at the table. Serafina could feel the girl's eyes on her as she poured her guest a cup of cider and sat down. The girl seemed agitated, and Serafina wanted to help her calm down before she asked her question. A few people were so nervous when they visited that it was hard to get a coherent question out of them, let alone the one they really wanted answered.

The girl picked up the cup, then set it down again without taking a sip. "My name is Dielle," the girl said, as if she could no longer stand the silence. "My mother's name is—"

"You don't need to tell me any names," said Serafina.

Dielle fidgeted with the cup, turning it around and around in her hands. "I know, but I thought it might make you want to help us if you knew more about us."

"I'll answer your question the same way whether I know anything about you or not. Go ahead, you can ask it now."

Dielle pushed the cup away. "As I said, my mother is very sick. She's getting worse every day. My father died when I was a baby, so it's just the two of us. I don't know what I'd do if . . ." Dielle swallowed hard and wiped her eyes with her knuckles. "What can I do to help my mother get better?"

"Go to see Doctor Tesar in Stary Smokevec," Serafina said in the voice that wasn't quite hers. "He knows of something that will help your mother live longer and in less pain. The doctor will ask for more gold than can be found in your entire village. Tell him that you don't have the gold, but that I sent you to him. Tell him I said that if he helps your mother, I will answer his question. If he does not, I will leave and he will never get the chance."

Dielle frowned in concentration. "I'll go today," she said. "Do you know where Stary Smokevec is?"

Serafina shook her head. "No, I don't. Sorry," she said in her own voice.

"Oh, right. That was my second question." Dielle stood with a sigh. "Thank you. Now I know what to do. I just have to find out how to get there."

Serafina got to her feet and crossed to her cupboard. "Here," she said, taking a few coins from her own supply. "You can use this to pay your way."

The girl smiled shyly as she took the coins. "Thank you!"

"I'm glad I could help," Serafina said, and watched as the girl opened the door and hurried to the gate.

* * *

72

It was less than a week later that Dielle was back, her footsteps lighter and her news good. The doctor had come to see her mother and given her a bottle of medicine that already seemed to be working. Dielle couldn't thank Serafina enough and brought her another bouquet of flowers.

Only two days after that, a fancy carriage that was ill-suited to traveling the narrow, uneven path rolled to a stop in front of Serafina's cottage. Serafina was outside when the carriage arrived. She watched as a footman jumped down and opened the door for a plump man wearing gold-colored leggings and a cape trimmed with fur. The man spoke to his coachman for a moment before turning to the cottage. He was halfway to the door when he noticed Serafina. Tilting his head back, he looked down his nose at her, taking in her poorly fitting gown.

"You may tell Baba Yaga that Doctor Tesar is here," he said, then turned away to examine the cottage.

Serafina's lips twisted in a wry smile as she strolled inside. She took her time brushing her hair and straightening her clothes before going to the door. "You may come in," she told the doctor, then turned her back on him and took her seat at the table, leaving him to shut the door. Not liking his manner, she saw no reason to be polite.

The doctor strode into the cottage and looked around, obviously expecting someone else to be there. He seemed surprised when he found that Serafina was alone.

"*I'm* Baba Yaga," she said. "What is your question?"

Ever since Dielle came to tell her about her mother's improving health, Serafina had been looking forward to the doctor's visit. She had convinced herself that a dedicated doctor would ask her something important, like how to cure a wasting sickness or repair a damaged heart, so she wasn't prepared when the doctor said, "My father hid all his gold shortly before he died. Where did he put it?"

It was the kind of question that she had been asked many times and had answered without thinking, only now as she answered she couldn't help but feel disappointed.

"He didn't hide it," she replied in her Baba Yaga voice. "He invested it in the cargo on a sailing ship. He died before the ship returned. Go see Captain Dolinski docked at Drapno Bay and take proof that you are your father's son. The captain has your father's money and will give it to you once he knows that you are the right man."

It was only after the doctor had gone, riding away in his rattling, jostling carriage, that she realized he hadn't brought a gift. *He probably thought that helping Dielle's mother was enough*, she thought, and decided that it was.

That very night another man came to see her, bringing a bottle of wine as his gift. A partially shuttered lantern swung wildly in his hand, the light jerking across the trees, the ground, and the sky as he stumbled and cursed.

Serafina had just gone to bed when she saw the erratic light through her window, but she didn't get up until she heard the person at the gate, trying to force it open. She was putting on her everyday gown again when she heard Boris yell, "Go away! Come back to see her when you're sober!"

"I brought her stupid gift and my question. I have as much right as anyone to hear her answer! Get the ugly old bat out here so I can ask my question, or I'll smash you to bits!" the man shouted.

Angry, Serafina threw the door open and stepped outside. "What is it that you have to ask in the middle of the night?"

The man raised his lantern until its light fell on her face, making her blink and look away. He didn't seem to notice that she was neither old nor ugly. "Invite me in first," he said, waving the half-empty bottle of wine in the air.

"I will not," she told him. "Ask your question so you can be on your way."

Taking a long swig from the bottle, the man staggered against the gate, making it creak alarmingly. "What I want to know is this," he said, wiping his mouth with the back of his hand. "My wife just gave birth to a boy with red hair. No one in my family has red hair. Is the boy mine?"

The last thing Serafina wanted to do was talk to this man, but there was no stopping the Baba Yaga voice. "No," she said, regretting the words she could not stop. "He is the son of the miller, who would be a better father than you ever will."

The man's voice drowned out her last words as he cursed at the top of his lungs. Flinging the nearly empty bottle at the door, he shouted, "Here's your blasted gift! You and your questions! I wish I'd never asked you! You shouldn't be allowed to answer questions like that! Maybe I should come in there and make sure you can never talk again! Open this blasted gate, and I'll—"

Serafina stepped back into her house and slammed the door. She felt something bump into her legs and glanced down to see Maks, his eyes glittering in the moonlight that came through the window. "Tell the cottage to go," said the cat.

"What are you talking about?" she asked over the roar of the man's voice.

"Tell the cottage to go *now*!" Maks shouted as the skulls screamed at the man.

"But Boris—"

"Will be fine if you do this!" said the cat. "Just say, 'Chicken hut, chicken hut, take me away,' and it will."

"All right! I . . ." Serafina took a deep breath, then said in a rush of words, "Chicken hut, chicken hut, take me away!"

The cottage vibrated like a dog shaking itself after a bath. Beams creaked and floorboards groaned as the structure lurched to one side, then the other. Serafina grabbed hold of the back of a chair and held on. The cottage rose abruptly, and the man's shouted curses became screams of terror. With a loud *thwack* the door flew open, allowing the stream of bones and skulls to rush through the doorway and down into their trunk. When the last bone had clattered in and the trunk lid had closed itself, the door slammed shut and the cottage began its swaying walk. Although the furniture didn't move, small objects did. The book was the only thing on the table that didn't budge. Everything else slid off the side and fell to the floor. A cup shattered, Serafina's hairbrush skated under the bed, and her shawl slithered across the wood planks until it snagged on the leg of a chair.

"The cottage shares a bond with each Baba Yaga and will listen to what you say. Next time, tell it to be careful when it gets up," said Maks. "It will if you tell it to, and we won't get rattled around like beetles in a nutshell."

"I'll remember that," Serafina said as she began to clean up the shattered cup. She was shaken, not only by the movement of the cottage but by the things the man had said to her. If only she could avoid answering certain kinds of questions!

Serafina worried deep into the night about what was going to happen to the man's wife and her baby and didn't go to sleep until it was nearly morning.

CHAPTER 8

When the cottage finally settled down, it was on the outskirts of a prosperous town. From the very first day, a steady stream of visitors came to ask their questions. There were so many that after a while they all began to run together in Serafina's mind. One morning, she was cleaning up after her breakfast when she noticed that Maks was licking his paw and scrubbing his face with it. She laughed suddenly, startling the cat.

"What's wrong with you?" asked Maks.

"Nothing," Serafina said. "I just remembered that a neighbor of mine always told us to expect guests when a cat washes his face. With all the guests we've had, you must have been washing your face a lot!"

Maks twitched his tail. "I don't think my bathing habits have anything to do with it!"

They both turned their heads at a knock on the door. Serafina gave the cat a questioning look. "You don't suppose . . . ," she began.

"It's just a coincidence!" said the cat as he jumped onto a trunk to look out the window. "Your friend has come to see you again," he announced.

"What friend?" Serafina said, even as she went to the door. When she opened it, Dielle was there, holding a single white daisy. "It's you!" Serafina said in surprise. "I didn't expect to see you again."

"I came to town to get more medicine for Mother," Dielle said, handing the daisy to Serafina. "When I heard that you were here, I thought I'd stop by."

"I'm glad you did! Usually my only visitors are people coming to ask a question."

Dielle went straight to the table and sat down. "Then it's about time you had a friend come calling."

"Are we friends, then?" Serafina asked, sounding wistful.

"Of course!" said Dielle. "You helped Mother and me more than anyone else ever did, and you can't tell me you did it for the flowers. We both count you as a friend now. I just hope that someday you'll get to meet Mother, too."

"I'd like that very much," Serafina said. "Which would you prefer, tea or cider?"

"Cider, if you don't mind."

"How is your mother?" Serafina asked as she took two cups from the cupboard.

"The same," said Dielle. "Which is better than she was before she got the medicine. Tell me something. Why do you look so much older than when I saw you last? It's been only a few weeks."

Serafina shrugged. "It's part of being Baba Yaga. I answer a question, my body gets older." Setting the two filled cups on the table, she sat down across from Dielle.

"Really?" said Dielle. "I never would have guessed! How did you end up being Baba Yaga? It's not a family thing, is it?"

"My great-aunt was the last Baba Yaga, but I think she gave me the job because she heard somehow that I could read and write, and thought I would be a good fit."

"You can read and write! I wish I could. Can you do anything else magic, besides answer questions? I mean, things that only a Baba Yaga can do."

"That's pretty much it. Except, well, I can tell the cottage to move."

"That's amazing! I bet you meet a lot of interesting people."

"Every day," said Serafina. "But you're the only friend who comes to see me. Aside from the people coming to ask me questions, the cat and the skulls are generally the only ones I have to talk to. Oh, and then there are the fairies . . . I never knew they were real until I became Baba Yaga. I think I can see them *because* I'm Baba Yaga. Why, the first time I saw them—"

"You've *seen* fairies?" Dielle asked, her eyes wide.

Serafina nodded. "A couple of times. They're very shy."

"Where do you see them? Are there any here now?"

Serafina laughed. "No, I don't see them now and I don't see them very often. When I do, it's only when I'm outside."

"Then let's go out!" Dielle said, hopping to her feet. "I'd love to see a fairy! Maybe if I'm with you when you see one, I'll see it, too!"

"All right," Serafina said, laughing, "but give me a minute to finish my cider!"

"You can take it with you!" Dielle said, herding her toward the door. "Here, I'll take mine, too. We can drink while we're walking." Snatching her mug from the table, Dielle hustled Serafina out of the cottage.

"I don't think fairies like to go where there are lots of people," Serafina said, glancing in the town's direction.

"Then we'll go the other way," said Dielle, turning toward the woods. "We'll find a place that the fairies would like."

They took a well-traveled path into the woods, then followed a deer trail until they reached a meadow filled with wildflowers. "This looks like a good place, wouldn't you say?" Dielle said, climbing onto a big rock.

"I'd like this spot if I were a fairy," said Serafina. She had already finished the cider in her mug and was thirsty from their hike, so when she saw a sparkling brook at the edge of the meadow, she knelt down to fill her mug, then did the same for Dielle.

"Do you see any fairies?" Dielle asked, looking at Serafina expectantly.

"Not yet," Serafina answered with a laugh. "But I do hear voices."

Dielle cocked her head to the side and listened. "I do, too," she said with a sigh. "I don't think we went far enough into the woods."

Serafina wandered toward the sound. Soon the trees thinned out, revealing two men and a wooden boat on the shore of a lake. One of the men was seated in the boat, while the other stood with one foot in the boat and the other on the bank. The man in the boat was struggling with the oars as the boat drifted away from shore.

Serafina heard Dielle come up behind her as the legs of the man who was standing spread farther and farther apart. Suddenly he fell in with a splash, his arms and legs thrashing.

Serafina started to laugh, and when she turned to Dielle, she found her friend laughing so hard that the water she had just sipped from her mug was coming out her nose. The two friends staggered away from the lake, collapsing on the edge of the meadow, where they laughed at the man falling into the water, at the sounds they made when they laughed, and for the sheer joy of laughing.

"My sides hurt," Dielle moaned, wrapping her arms around her stomach.

"So do mine," Serafina gasped. She squeezed her eyes shut and took great shuddering breaths. When she opened her eyes, she was facing a yellow blossom bending so low it almost touched her face. A tiny man with pale green wings sat astride the blossom, watching her.

Serafina tried not to move, not wanting to frighten him. "Dielle," she whispered.

"What?" Dielle asked, and hiccuped loudly.

The fairy shot into the air. His wings were just a blur when he flew away.

"Did you see him?" Serafina asked, sitting up and turning to face her friend.

"Who, the man in the boat or the one in the water?" Dielle asked, giggling. "Please, don't get me started again!"

"Never mind," Serafina said as she got to her feet. Somehow she couldn't bring herself to tell Dielle that she had just missed seeing a fairy.

They headed back to Serafina's cottage. When they reached the gate, Dielle handed her mug to Serafina saying, "I should go now. Mother will be wondering what happened to me. I'll come see you again when I can. I don't suppose you know where you'll be in a few weeks?"

"I don't know where I'll be from one day to the next," said Serafina, "but come visit anytime!"

"I will," said Dielle. "I promise!"

*　*　*

The next three days were hectic, with more people coming to see Serafina than ever before. She was thinking about going for a short walk one day, just to get a break, when she heard Boris arguing with someone at the gate.

"No, I'm not going to let you in without announcing you. She's in charge here, not you! Baba Yaga! There's someone here to— Ow! Stop hitting me, old woman!"

Serafina peeked out the window to see an old woman

rap the skull with her cane. The gate swung wide, even though Boris was gnashing his teeth at their visitor. Serafina opened the door just as the woman stomped into the yard.

"If it isn't the new little Baba Yaga!" the stranger said, sneering. "I never thought I'd have a question for you, but then we live in unpredictable times, more's the pity. Invite me inside, girl. There are too many prying eyes out here!"

"Please come in," Serafina said, stepping aside to let the woman past.

Leaning on her cane, the old woman hobbled across the threshold and paused to examine the room. Her nearly black eyes glittered when she took a seat at the table without being asked. Bits of dried grass and twigs stuck out of her filthy long gray hair, whose tangles had knots as big as her fist. One of the knots moved, and bright, beady eyes peered out at Serafina. When the old woman rested her arm on the table, tiny spiders leaked from her sleeve and skittered away. Serafina tried not to wrinkle her nose at the smell that enveloped the woman. It was a heavy smell, like dead mice rotting in the walls of an old house; Serafina wondered if she'd ever be able to get rid of the odor.

The woman's eyes darted here and there as if she

was appraising everything. Even when sitting, she was in constant motion, her fingers thrumming the table. She was just turning toward Serafina when Maks growled at something outside the door.

The old woman had a string tied to her finger, and she'd begun to reel it in with her other hand. The string ran across the floor and out the door. As it shortened, it dragged something kitten-sized with matted fur and tiny red eyes over the threshold and across the cottage floor. Maks spit and snarled, swiping at its back without actually touching it. The little animal turned to snap at the cat, revealing sharp, pointed teeth almost too big for its mouth. Serafina could hear Mak's low growl as he trailed the creature across the room.

Suddenly the little animal jumped, landing on the old woman's lap. Reaching into her pocket, the woman pulled out something long and skinny. The creature began to gnaw on it, growling and making slobbery sounds as it chewed. Serafina took a step back when she realized that it was eating an old, dried finger.

"What did you want to ask me?" Serafina asked the woman.

"Aren't you one for getting right to the point!" said the woman. "No social niceties here! Fine, be that way. I came to ask you a question and ask I will, but I'll say what I've got to say first. I've lived in the same house just outside Vioska for forty-seven years, and in all that time, my neighbors have learned to leave me alone. We have our occasional tiffs—they wonder where their lost relatives have gone and come nosing around my house, though they've never found anything, I've made sure of that! And when I need a few ingredients for my work, I sometimes go to them, stingy as they are. All in all, however, we've left one another alone. Until now, that is. It seems they have a new sheriff whose nose is bent out of shape over a few missing people. I could have stayed, of course, but they were planning to burn me at the stake, so I slipped away in the middle of the night. Only now I don't have anywhere to go. So here's my question—where can I go that I can scare people into letting me do what I want and they won't be able to do a thing about it?"

Serafina didn't want to answer this woman or help her in any way. Even though she tried to keep her mouth closed, her lips parted of their own accord, and she said in her Baba Yaga voice, "In the kingdom of Norovise lies a small village called Pimki. Most of the young people have moved away, leaving only the infirm and elderly. No one who currently resides in Pimki can stand against you."

The old woman's eyes lit up. She licked her lips and stood, dumping her odd pet onto the floor. Moving toward the door, the woman dragged the creature on the string, pausing just inside the threshold to size up Serafina. "You don't look like much, but it occurs to me that you might tell someone where I've gone. By all rights I should kill you. I won't, however, because I've heard that anyone who kills the Baba Yaga becomes the next Baba Yaga, and I'm not about to get stuck with the job. I know I'm supposed to give you a gift, so consider your life my gift. If you're smart, you'll keep your mouth shut and not tell anyone about me."

The woman paused, still staring at Serafina. "Hmm. You don't look that smart to me, so perhaps I should take one little precaution." Pulling a crooked stick from the folds of her gown, she pointed it at Serafina and said, "If you tell anyone that I was here or the question that I asked, your tongue will shrivel in your mouth and you'll never be able to speak again."

"I won't," Serafina said, and waited until the old woman had gone before adding, "unless someone asks me."

* * *

After the witch's visit, dozens of people came to see Serafina, but she waited until a farmer who seemed honest and reliable stopped by before mentioning that the sheriff of Vioska should come to see her. It wasn't until the end of the week, when she'd almost given up hope, that the sheriff finally appeared.

"I hear that you want to see me," the sheriff said, laying his cap on the table as he took a seat. From the condition of the horse he'd left tethered to the gate, it appeared that the man had ridden long and hard to get to her, and he looked grateful when she handed him a cup of cold cider. She couldn't help noticing that he was only a few years older than Alek.

"I do, indeed," Serafina said as she took the seat across from him. "I understand that you've had a problem."

Ever since she mentioned the sheriff to the farmer, Serafina hadn't slept well. Visions of her tongue shriveling in her mouth had haunted her dreams, and she frequently found herself pressing her tongue against her teeth and swiping it across her palate. She had no control over what the sheriff might ask; if he asked the wrong question, she fully believed that her tongue would shrivel in her mouth. If only she could just tell the sheriff where the witch had gone without saying anything else, but she was afraid that he'd ask if the old woman had visited the cottage. Serafina's Baba Yaga voice might then tell him precisely what the witch had warned her not to say. Even though she feared the curse, Serafina couldn't let the witch do what she had planned. People's lives depended on the sheriff knowing where the witch had gone.

The sheriff took a sip of his cider, watching her over the rim of the cup. When he set it down, he nodded and said, "We were about to capture a nasty witch when she suddenly disappeared." His eyes narrowed as he looked at Serafina. "I've heard that you can answer one question with the truth. I know what my question should be. Where did the witch go?"

Serafina sighed with relief. She wouldn't have to tell him that the witch had been there or repeat the question that she had asked, either of which would have withered Serafina's tongue. "The witch has only recently arrived in a small village called Pimki, in the kingdom of Norovise," she said in her Baba Yaga voice. "Most of the young people have moved away, leaving only the infirm and elderly. No one who currently resides in Pimki can stand against the witch. She will be complacent now and not expecting a young sheriff to lead a score of armed men to capture and gag her before she can cast a spell that would allow her to escape."

The sheriff listened intently while she was talking. When she was done, he drained the cup of cider and set it on the table. "I must be off," he said, picking up his cap. "It seems I'll be traveling with some friends."

"I wish you luck," Serafina said, following him to the door.

"And I thank you for your help," he said, bowing to her as if she were a grand lady at court.

Serafina smiled as the sheriff walked away. The people of Pimki would soon be safe, and she might be able to get a good night's sleep now that she knew she was keeping her tongue.

CHAPTER 9

Two weeks later, a messenger arrived at the cottage, bringing a note and a small leather pouch for Serafina. He had already ridden off by the time Serafina opened the note and read:

> BABA YAGA,
>
> AFTER I MET YOU, I LEARNED THAT I
> SHOULD HAVE GIVEN YOU A GIFT WHEN I ASKED
> YOU MY QUESTION. HERE IS THE GIFT, ALONG
> WITH MY THANKS. WE CAUGHT THE WITCH!
> TOMAN DAMEK, SHERIFF OF VIOSKA

Serafina untied the string holding the pouch shut and shook a lovely gold brooch into her hand. She admired it for a moment before tucking the brooch back in the pouch. It was probably very expensive, but the only piece of jewelry that really mattered was the heart that Alek had given to her. The brooch was just payment for information.

Placing her hand on her chest, Serafina felt the gold heart she wore hidden under the neck of her gown. It meant more to her than just a piece of jewelry; it was a sign of how much Alek loved her. Remembering the look on his face when he gave her the token, she felt a pang of longing and tears sprang to her eyes. If only she could see him again!

Serafina was still standing in the doorway, her gaze fixed on the swaying barley growing in the field across the road, when Maks sauntered out of the cottage and rubbed against her legs. When she didn't respond, he peered up at her and asked, "What's wrong with you?"

"I'm never going to get free of being Baba Yaga, am I?" she asked. "The rest of my life is going to be just like this. I'll spend my days waiting for strangers to show up, knowing that it's probably the only time I'll ever see them. I'll never again have people I can love or who will love me. And just look at me. I don't even need a mirror to know that I'm getting old. My hands look like my grandmother's, and I'm getting pains in places that never hurt before. This can't last very long, now, can it? If I have to answer questions and age each time I do, my life is going to be awfully short."

"Why?" asked Maks, who was watching a butterfly flit across the yard. "All you have to do is drink the tea."

Serafina turned to face him. "What tea?"

"Ask the book how you can be young again," said the cat, and he scampered out the open door.

Serafina was muttering to herself about all the things she'd like to do to unhelpful cats when she sat down at the table and reached for the book. Flipping through to the first blank page, she cleared her throat and said, "I get older every time I answer a question. How can I be young again?"

As the words appeared on the parchment, Serafina leaned closer and read:

Drink the blue rose tea.

"Where can I find this tea?" she asked, but no other words appeared. Something niggled at the back of her mind—she was sure she'd seen something some-where. If only she could remember.

Serafina let her gaze wander around the room. Where would she put something that she wanted to keep really safe? Although the cupboard was an obvious place to keep tea, would the other Baba Yagas have kept such a special tea with the rest of the food? She'd been drinking some of the herbal teas, but visitors she had spoken with herself had brought most of them and she knew none of those teas included roses in their mixtures.

Serafina sorted through the shelf that held the old teas first. She found more herbal teas, a small pot of dried dandelions for dandelion tea, some shriveled dried things that smelled vaguely like blueberries, and an old bag of rose hip tea that was moldy and smelled bad when she opened it. There wasn't much of it, but she had no way of knowing if it had been made with blue roses or roses of a more conventional color, so she set it aside, hoping that it wasn't what she needed.

The next shelf down was filled with small sacks of barley flour, wheat flour, and oats. She threw out a sack of ancient dried apples and was about to go to the next shelf when she spied a clay jar with a cork crammed into the opening. Although she had seen it before, she had no idea what was in it. Someone had labeled it at some point, but the writing was in a language she didn't

96

understand. Turning it over in her hands, she was delighted when she found "Blue Rose Tea" written in a different script at the bottom.

It didn't take long to make herself a cup of tea. When it was ready, she sat at the table with the cup and the mirror in front of her. If she was going to change, she wanted to see it happen.

After taking the first sip, she stared at her reflection in the mirror, but as far as she could tell, she looked just the same. The tea was muskier than she'd expected and left a strange aftertaste in her mouth. If she had been drinking it just because she was thirsty, she probably wouldn't have had any more, but she wasn't drinking it for the taste. She took a second sip.

The tingling started in her fingertips first. She sat back and stared at her hands as the feeling traveled past her knuckles to her wrists and up her arms, making the fine hairs stand on end. The skin grew tauter, and the spots that had appeared on the back of her hands over the last few days disappeared. She took another sip, then another and another, until the cup was empty. In only a few minutes, the tingling engulfed her entire body. When it reached her face, she leaned toward the mirror and watched as the lines beside her eyes and mouth vanished, her skin grew firmer, her eyes grew brighter, and her hair became darker and more lustrous. When the tingling finally stopped, she realized that all her aches and pains were gone. She was young again, though she thought she looked a little older than she had when she first became Baba Yaga.

Sitting back in her seat, Serafina closed her eyes and reveled in the sensations of being young and healthy. Now she didn't have to die of old age before she was even fifteen. And there was plenty of tea in the jar. If she was careful with it, the tea should last her a long time.

Serafina did a little dance when she stood. Her lithe young body could move easily, and the freedom of movement made her so happy that she hummed a merry tune as she began to clean up. After pushing the cork back in the jar, she returned the tea to the cupboard where she had found it, then washed her cup. She was putting it away when something else occurred to her. Now she looked nearly the same as she had before she became Baba Yaga. She could go home and if she told everyone not to ask her questions, she could even have the life she wanted! If she hurried, she could be back with her family soon.

Serafina was so excited that she almost blurted out the command, but even as she opened her mouth, she recalled what had happened the last time she told the cottage to move. This time she remembered to say, "Chicken hut, chicken hut, take me home, but do it gently!"

The cottage rose so smoothly that she barely felt as if it was moving at all. The door was already open when the fence came apart, and the bones flew into the cottage, bringing the skulls with them. Yowling, Maks followed them into the air and through the doorway, landing on the bed.

"What are you doing?" demanded the cat. "You made me drop a nice juicy mouse!"

"We're going home," said Serafina.

"You could have given me some warning! You look good, by the way. I guess you found the tea."

"No thanks to you," Serafina told him.

"What can I say? I'm a cat. What did you mean when you said we were going home? We already are home."

"I mean my hometown, Kamien Dom. Wait until you meet my family! They've never met a talking cat before. And Alek—"

"I doubt we're going to your hometown," said Maks. "Old Chicken Legs is a cottage of habit. It likes to go to the same places and rarely goes anywhere new. Most of the places it visits now meant something impor-tant to the first Baba Yaga. That was so long ago that whatever was there might be gone by now, but it goes there anyway. Something pretty powerful is needed to make this hut go someplace different; just asking isn't going to do it. What did you say to it?"

"I told it to take me home," Serafina said, no longer feeling quite so excited.

"Then I bet it's taking us to Mala Kapusta. That's where it picked you up. It's probably the closest stop to your village."

"I live in a large town, actually," Serafina said.

"Well, there you have it! This cottage never goes to large towns. Too many people around. Even in the villages, the cottage times its arrival for after dark so it's already in place when people get up in the morning. Fewer terrified villagers running and screaming that way. The villagers are used to seeing it, just not the way it walks around on chicken legs. Departures can be a different story, though. Sometimes we have to leave in a hurry, and everyone gets riled up."

"Chicken legs?" asked Serafina.

Maks gave his paw an experimental lick. "Uh-huh," he said. "I'm surprised you haven't noticed its footprints. Of course, they are big. Look more like ruts than the footprints of a chicken." The cat gave his paw another swipe with his tongue, then glanced up at her. "I told you that the first Baba Yaga was a nasty old witch. Long before the fairy put the curse on her, she got into trouble with some villagers. She heard that they were coming to burn her hut, so she grabbed the only animal she could find at the time and used it in a spell. It was a scrawny old chicken, too tough even for the old witch to eat. The spell put the chicken legs on the hut and made them big enough to carry the hut around."

"So that's why it lurches the way it does," Serafina said. "I guess it's a good thing she didn't find a frog, or we'd be hopping everywhere."

Maks licked his shoulder, then glanced up at Serafina again. "Hey, I'm glad I wasn't living with her then, or it might have been my legs that were hauling this thing!" Turning to look over his back, he twitched his tail when he noticed that his fur was ruffled and dirty. "Promise me one thing. The next time you want to pick up and leave, tell me first!"

* * *

It was still dark when the cottage settled to the ground. Woken from her sleep, Serafina climbed out of bed and slipped into her prettiest gown. Her heart sang as she brushed her hair until it shone. She was going home today and would see Alek and her family!

101

Maks watched from the bed while she pulled on her shoes, and she half expected him to try to talk her out of going. He didn't, though, and when she bent down to pet his head, he stood and stalked away.

The sun was just starting to come up when Serafina stepped outside, the few coins she possessed in her pocket. It had been dark the last time she was there, but as far as she could tell, the cottage had come back to the very same place she and Viktor had found it.

"Where are you going so early?" called one of the skulls as Serafina headed for the gate.

"To stretch my legs," she replied, not wanting to tell them that she was leaving for good. She liked the skulls, but she didn't feel like explaining herself to anyone; she certainly didn't want to argue about it.

"Hurry back," Boris said as she closed the gate behind her.

Serafina patted the shiny skull and turned toward the Bialy Jelen tavern. If anyone could tell her how she could get a ride to Kamien Dom, it would be a tavern keeper.

Although it was still early, the day promised to be beautiful. The sky was clear and a gentle breeze already carried a hint of warmth. Serafina felt more lighthearted than she had since the day she received her great-aunt's letter. Grinning, she started skipping down the road, something she hadn't done in years. She stopped, however, when she heard someone chuckle.

A man leading a horse from behind the tavern tipped his hat to her and said, "Good morning, miss. And how are you today?"

"Very well," Serafina said, and went rigid when she realized that she'd said it in her Baba Yaga voice.

The man nodded and continued on, but Serafina didn't budge. She had felt her clothes tighten just as they had when she first became Baba Yaga. There was no getting away from what had happened to her. Even simple questions made her age. If she went home, people were bound to ask her questions; they would just slip out, unintentionally. She would age then, surrounded by her family and friends. It would be impossible to hide what was happening to her unless she drank the tea every day, and she doubted she had enough to do that for long.

Serafina could only imagine what having someone like her in the household would do to her family. They didn't believe in magic, so how could they accept what had happened to her? It was likely that her parents would think she had some awful aging disease and want to find her a cure. If she insisted that it was due to magic, any doctor they called in would probably label her crazy and suggest that they lock her away somewhere.

And what about Alek? Even if he did believe that magic was behind it, once he saw how she aged after answering a question, he wouldn't want to marry her anymore. The thought of losing Alek's love was more than she could bear.

Serafina turned around and headed back to the cottage, her footsteps slow and dragging, as miserable now as she had been happy just minutes before.

It took her longer to return to the cottage than it had to reach the tavern, and her footsteps slowed even more the closer she drew. She had stopped in front of the gate when a cardinal darted past, the flash of red catching her eye so that she turned to watch it. The bird flew to the opposite side of the road where an old apple tree stood, its branches gnarled and drooping. Landing on a branch near a large, rounded hole in the trunk, the cardinal began to tug at something. It was a ribbon, dangling from the hole, and Serafina realized with surprise that it was the same unusual shade of blue as a ribbon that Alek had given her. "He always liked that color on me," she murmured, taking a step closer.

The cardinal flew off at her approach, having pulled

the ribbon further out of the hole. Serafina could see that the ribbon was attached to something. Curious, she tugged on it, and a withered bouquet fell to the ground. The flowers were roses, faded and dried, but she could tell that they had been pink. Pink roses were her favorite. When she picked up the bouquet, a note fell out, and she reached for that as well. She gasped when she read the single word on the back of the note. Written in familiar handwriting, it said *"Fina."*

She opened the note and her gaze flew to the bottom of the message. Her breath caught in her throat when she saw Alek's signature.

"What you got there?" called one of the skulls from across the road.

"A note for me," she said.

At the sound of an approaching wagon, Serafina hurried to the gate, the bouquet and note clutched in her hand.

"Aren't you going to tell us what it says?" asked Krany.

"It's her business, not yours," Yure told him. "She'll share it with us if she wants to, and since we're all friends—"

"Maybe later," Serafina told them, opening the cottage door.

"Back so soon?" Maks asked as she stepped inside.

"You need to go out," she told him. Placing her finds on the table, she picked up the cat and carried him to the door. He was squirming and protesting when she set him down, and he tried to run back in, but she pushed him away long enough to close the door behind him. "Sometimes a girl needs privacy," she murmured to herself, and turned back to the table.

Serafina carried the note to the bed and sat down. Tears welled in her eyes as she read Alek's words.

My darling Fina,

    After Viktor came home without you, telling a crazy story about a house that had carried you off, your father and Yevhen went to look for you and returned home heartbroken. When I finally heard about it, I hurried to Mala Kapusta to look for you myself. There was no trace of any house save for strange nuts in the ground, but the villagers swear that the house belonged to Baba Yaga, a woman who is sometimes old and sometimes young, who comes and goes in a house with chicken legs and who will tell you the truth when you ask her a question. No one had any idea why the old woman would carry you off, but they say that she will return someday.

I do not know if you are still with the old woman, but I hope and pray that she is keeping you safe and well and that you will find this note.

I love you, Serafina, and will never give up my search for you. We will be together again someday, I promise you.

Love,
Alek

Serafina sat for a time, reading the note over and over. When a headache began to form behind her eyes, she folded the note and tucked it in her pocket. Alek said that he still loved her, but then he had yet to learn that she was the new Baba Yaga. She wasn't the same innocent girl he had known. If he found out what had really happened to her, he would want to do something about it, and there was nothing anyone could do. It would be better if she left and never saw him again.

Serafina thought about writing Alek a note but couldn't bring herself to do it. Then the first visitor came to the door, and she spent the rest of the day answering questions. By the time night fell, all she wanted to do was leave, so once again she asked the cottage to stand up and walk away, which it did, leaving only its footprints behind.

CHAPTER 10

The next morning, Serafina opened the door to see where the cottage had settled. It was perched at the edge of the forest, high enough above the floor of a long valley that she could see for miles. Farmland blanketed the emerald-green valley all the way to the far end, where a city surrounded a castle bristling with turrets. Even from so far away she could see that something was going on. The road that passed in front of the city gates was congested with travelers. Light reflected off the polished armor of knights, and there seemed to be more people on horseback than she had ever seen in Kamien Dom. It was a beautiful view, but Serafina had no idea where she was.

A road that was little more than a goat path wound

out of the forest, looping in front of the cottage and back into the forest a few hundred feet away. Serafina doubted that it ever saw much traffic, but even so, she soon had her first visitor. After that, a steady stream of people coming to ask her questions kept her occupied for the rest of the day. A visitor woke her early the next morning, and the second person arrived soon after the first one left.

A week after her arrival she was sitting at her table, mending a torn sleeve, when she heard the tread of many feet. Peeking out her window, she saw that a mounted knight had arrived at her gate with a dozen foot soldiers. She wondered for a moment if she was in trouble or in some sort of danger and was reluctant to respond when the knight called out, "Baba Yaga!" It wasn't until he'd called a second time that she opened the door and stepped outside.

"What do you want of me?" she asked.

"If you are Baba Yaga, the woman who answers questions with the truth, answer 'yes,'" said the knight.

"Yes," she replied in her own voice. She expected him to come inside, but he turned his horse and rode back the way he had come, his soldiers following in his wake. "That's one way to get an answer without posing a real question," she murmured as he rode away.

The next morning, she had just finished her breakfast of oatmeal when she heard a distant rumble. Thinking that it was thunder, she glanced outside and was surprised to see that it was a beautiful day with only a few puffy clouds scudding high in the sky. She also saw that the skulls were all looking toward the city. Curious, she opened the door. The rumbling was suddenly much louder.

"What is it?" she asked the skulls as she peered at the cloud of dust crossing the valley floor.

"A small army is coming," Boris replied.

"I was in the army back when I was alive," Krany told them. "For a few weeks after, too. My buddies dragged me around with them until they found a good place to bury me. They finally dumped me in a hole when I got too ripe. That hole sure was cozy."

"Look at the crimson banners," said Boris. "That's the color of the kingdom of Vargas. I bet that's the king's own guard. We've been watching them ever since they left the castle."

"The king must be with them," said Yure. "Otherwise there wouldn't be so many."

"Tell me when they come out of the trees," Serafina told the skulls, and hurried back inside to tidy the cottage. After cleaning up her dishes, she made her bed and changed into the best gown she could find in the trunk. Her hair was thick with only a touch of gray, so she plaited it in a long braid like her mother usually wore. She was soon outside again and was waiting with the skulls when mounted men riding single file emerged from the forest carrying banners attached to long poles.

Although the king wasn't wearing a crown or clothes of state, she knew who he was by the respectful way the soldiers looked at him. Guards surrounded the king as he approached the cottage, and two came to the gate ahead of the rest.

"His Royal Majesty, King Borysko of Vargas, has come to speak with Baba Yaga," said the larger of the men, both of whom were dressed as officers.

"Only the person asking a question may enter," she told them.

"The king goes nowhere without his guard," said the officer as he set his hand on the finger-bone latch.

Serafina straightened her back and held her head high. A king had come to see her. As Serafina Divis, she would have been happy to usher them all inside, but he hadn't come to see Serafina. He had come to see Baba Yaga, a very special person who was also due respect.

"I'm sorry," she said. "It is one of my rules."

Serafina had turned as if to go back into the cottage

when a deep voice said behind her, "I will enter by myself."

Serafina glanced back at the gate. The king had come forward and was eyeing Boris, so she hurried to let him in before the skulls could say anything. Letting the king walk in front of her, she closed the gate, which made a loud click, and left the guards and the skulls watching one another.

"You're awfully young to be Baba Yaga," the king told her as she showed him to a seat at her table. "I expected to find an old crone, not a lovely woman."

"Sometimes I am older, sometimes I am younger," Serafina said, taking her normal seat. Although she knew that one was never supposed to sit in front of a king without permission, she figured that only Baba Yaga's rules applied inside the cottage.

The king nodded as if her statement made perfect sense, even though Serafina knew her explanation was lacking any logic.

"May I offer you some tea or cider?" she asked, trying to think of what her mother would do in this situation. When she thought of what her mother's face would look like if she knew her daughter was playing hostess to a king, she almost laughed out loud.

The king shook his head. "I just want my question

answered," he said, and proceeded to stare at his hands without speaking for so long that Serafina began to wonder what was wrong. "My advisors told me to be careful what I say in front of you," he finally said. "I must not ask you any questions until I ask the one I came to have answered. My wife's cousin is sheriff of Vioska, a minor post, but one good enough to test the mettle of an up-and-coming young man. He sent word of what you had done to help him rid the world of a particularly nasty witch. It occurred to me that I might make use of your ability as well. My question is simple enough, but much depends on your answer. If I declare war on my enemy, will I win?"

Serafina sat back and let the voice speak for her. "You will defeat your enemy, but in so doing will lose many of the people you hold most dear. Much of your kingdom will be destroyed, and you will be left the king of ruins."

The king looked solemn when he thanked her and bade her farewell. He left a sack of gold coins on the table when he stood and strode outside. Serafina overheard him talking to his officers who'd been waiting by the gate. He told them that he knew what he had to do; he would declare war as soon as he reached the castle.

Serafina stayed in her chair, too numb to move. She heard the gate open and close, then the king and his men ride away. Of all the terrible things she had had to tell anyone, she thought that this was the worst. The king had heard what she had to say, but her warnings had made no difference. He would win, that was all that mattered, even though many of his subjects would die in the war and his kingdom would be changed forever. Serafina had never felt so awful.

Vargas, a neighbor of Pazurskie, was a peaceful kingdom. Unfortunately, King Kolenka of Khrebek, the kingdom just north of Vargas, was hungry to expand his reign. If Vargas was going to war, King Kolenka must have done something that King Borysko could not ignore. Even so, whether it was justified or not, war was a terrible thing.

* * *

As word spread that the kingdom was at war, more and more people came to see her. The tenor of the questions changed, and people rarely received good news. Nearly everyone who came to her door wanted to know how their family would fare or if they themselves would live. A few wanted to know how they could survive the war. Even fewer were given helpful answers.

Late one afternoon, a young man came to the gate carrying a sleeping baby. Without saying a word, he entered the cottage and took the offered chair, still cradling the infant in his arms. The man's face was pale and he licked his lips nervously, but his hand was steady when he placed a loaf of bread still warm from the oven on the table.

"I was supposed to take this home for my family, but I'd heard we should bring a gift to get an answer from you. My daughter is four days old, and my wife is too ill to get out of bed. My father says that I must go to the castle in the morning and take up arms for the king. My wife doesn't want me to go. She said she had a vision that I was going to die. Was her vision right?"

Serafina straightened her back and took a deep breath. She hated answering questions like this, but she had no choice. "Yes, it was. In two months' time an enemy's arrow will strike you down."

"But my family needs me! Isn't there anything I can do?"

"I wish I could tell you, but I can answer only your first question," Serafina told him in her own voice.

"Yes, but this is important. Surely you can make an exception! I can't leave my family now. If I don't join the king's army, will I die in two months regardless of what I do? What if I take my family and leave the kingdom? I have an uncle in—"

"I'm sorry, but I really don't have any more answers for you."

The young man gave her a disgusted look. "That's what you say, but I bet you could if you wanted to. What is it? The bread wasn't enough? If I brought you gold, you'd answer all my questions, wouldn't you?"

"No, I wouldn't," Serafina said, getting to her feet. "The gifts my visitors bring have no influence on the answers I give them. I can tell the truth for one question from each person, and that is all. After that, I know no more how to answer their questions than they would themselves."

"Then what good are you?" the young man said, shouldering the baby so that she woke and began to cry. He stood and started toward the door, but before he reached it he paused long enough to turn to Serafina. "I wish I'd never come here. At least then I'd still have hope."

Serafina didn't know what to say. She watched him go, feeling less than useless as the young father walked away. When he reached the forest, she closed the door and drifted back to her seat at the table. Seeing the bread he'd brought, she thought about giving it back to him, but he was already gone and she didn't think he'd want to see her again.

She went to bed early that night. Lying on her back with the covers pulled up to her chin, she thought about the young man and how hopeless he must feel. Other people had asked when they were going to die, even more often since the king declared war than in all the rest of the days that she'd been Baba Yaga, but no one else had made her feel so terrible. It was horrible news for the ones who were going to die soon, but she didn't think even the people who were going to live a long time should ask the question. Knowing when one would die was bound to change one's life. If only she could pick and choose which questions she would answer!

When Maks jumped onto the bed, Serafina rolled onto her side. "Are you still awake?" he asked.

"I can't sleep. The last few days have been dreadful and tomorrow won't be any better. The king declared war because of something I said, so I feel as if I should stay to see these people through whatever comes. But the answers I have to give them are so awful!"

"The king didn't declare war because of you," said Maks. "You just told him what would happen if he did fight. He probably had his mind made up before he ever came here." The cat curled up against Serafina's back and nudged her with his nose. "Why do you think the people need you? What good can you do them by answering their questions now?"

"That young man said that I wasn't doing any good. He was probably right."

The moon was high in the sky when Serafina crawled out of bed to put away all the loose objects. Maks yawned and stretched his legs in front of him. "What are you doing?" he asked.

"Getting ready to go," Serafina told him. "I can't talk to one more person in this kingdom. I need to hear from someone who actually likes me. Chicken hut, chicken hut!" she cried. "Be careful when you stand and take me to Mala Kapusta. There might be a letter waiting there for me. And maybe this time I'll send some back."

CHAPTER 11

Serafina wrote a letter to her parents while the cottage lurched across the countryside. It was a difficult letter to write because she still wasn't sure how much to tell them. How did you inform people that magic had changed you when they were adamant that they didn't believe in magic? She finally settled on telling them only what she had to.

> Dear Mother and Father,
>   I hope you are well. I am fine and living in
> Great-Aunt Sylanna's cottage. Sylanna was
> mortally ill and went away before I arrived,
> leaving me to handle her responsibilities. Her cat
> is keeping me company and I am meeting new

people every day. A few days ago I actually
talked to a king!

I am sorry that I cannot come home now.
Please give my love to Alina and Katya.

Love,
Fina

The second letter she wrote was to Alek. She wasn't
happy that she had told her parents so little and hoped
that Alek would fill in the gaps. Hearing in person that
magic was real had to be better than reading it in
a letter.

Dear Alek,

Thank you for finding a way to get letters
to me. I am well and living in my great-aunt
Sylanna's cottage with her cat. Since my arrival,
I have learned that magic, fairies, and so many
things we never would have thought possible are
actually real. This cottage even moves when I tell
it to!

I never did meet Sylanna, but I've learned
that a fairy took her somewhere beautiful to live out
her last days. I've received my inheritance. I'm
the new Baba Yaga, something I never believed

really existed until now. I don't know how long I have to be Baba Yaga, but I do know that I can't walk away from it, no matter how much I wish I could.

My family will have a hard time accepting what has happened to me, so I hope that you will explain it to them and help them understand that I am fine, although unable to come home yet. They don't believe in magic and will be hard to convince. Getting them to accept that magic is real may be the hardest part of telling them about my new life.

Please don't worry about me, Alek. My life isn't what I want it to be, but it isn't horrible either. I meet new people and see new places all the time. I even met a king the other day! You know how much I like to learn new things. My goal now is to learn how to stop being Baba Yaga so that I can come home.

I miss you, Alek, and think about you all the time. Please write again when you can.

Love,
Fina

As the cottage settled to the ground, Serafina glanced out the window and was relieved to see that they had indeed come to Mala Kapusta. Hoping to find another bouquet in the tree, she gathered the letters she'd written and hurried outside. Her heart beat faster as she reached into the hole, and she gasped when her fingers closed on flower stems. Alek had written to her again!

After leaving her own letters in the hollow tree, she was on her way back to the cottage with the bouquet and Alek's letter when she heard the clash of metal on metal and men shouting in the town. Turning to look, she saw men fighting farther down the street.

"Get inside!" shouted Boris.

"What is it?" she asked as she hurried to the gate.

"It looks like the war has come here, too," Krany said as soldiers on lathered horses raced past the cottage into town. "Evil spreads faster than good, like my grandmother used to say."

The fighting was drawing closer when Serafina slipped inside the cottage and shut the door. "Chicken hut, chicken hut, take me away from here!" she cried, and threw herself onto the bed.

A cup fell off the table and shattered when the cottage lurched from side to side. The shouting outdoors grew louder, and Serafina wondered if the men had seen the cottage move. But then she forgot all about them as she opened the note from Alek.

My Darling Fina,

Someone took my last note—I hope that it was you. I am placing another in the tree and will continue to put them there until the day we are together again. Please let me know that you have received my message.

I have learned more about Baba Yaga. An old woman told me that once in every generation, Baba Yaga must find her replacement. The old woman believes that because Baba Yaga sent for you, you are that replacement.

Everyone here is fine. I go to see your family often. Alina had her baby! It is a boy and they have named him Osip. When I held him the other day, he spit up all over me. He smiled and seemed very pleased with himself, but they told me it was just gas. Widow Zloto visits your parents every day. She tells us that she has befriended a poor hatmaker and is buying his hats to help him out. The hats are awful and she is wearing a new one every time I see her.

*Do not despair, Fina. I am not going to give up!
We will be together again! If there is a way to get
you back, I am going to find it!*

                                        Love,
                                        Alek

Tears blurred her eyes as Serafina read the note a second time, then a third. Alina had given birth to her baby! Serafina had promised to be there to help out, and now she didn't know if she'd ever even see the little one. If only Sylanna had never sent her that letter!

As for Alek, she'd always known that he was stubborn and she didn't doubt for an instant that he would keep looking for her no matter what. At first the knowledge that he cared so much for her made her feel warm and good inside, but then she began to wonder if she really wanted him to keep looking. She loved him as much as he loved her, but she wanted him to be happy, not doomed to a life of seeking something he couldn't have.

Serafina read the note once more as the cottage settled into a rolling gait. She was used to it now and even found it soothing, so it wasn't long before she dozed off with the parchment crumpled in her hand.

* * *

When the cottage finally stopped walking, it was in the middle of the woods near the site of an abandoned village. Serafina wondered what had happened to everyone, but she enjoyed the peace and quiet for a change. Over the next few days, only a few people found their way to the cottage, giving Serafina plenty of time to think about Alek. She would start a chore that didn't require any thought, like polishing the skulls or feeding the cat, and find herself thinking about the way Alek had teased her about baiting her hook with worms the last time they went fishing or the face he'd made when he tried a piece of cooked eel but ate it anyway just to be polite. She missed him so much that an empty spot inside her chest ached when she thought of him.

Serafina also thought about what she should write to him in her next letter. Should she encourage him, telling him how much she wanted to be with him and that she hoped he would indeed find a way for them to be together? Or maybe she should write back to tell him that she wanted him to forget about her and move on with his life. She could tell him that she didn't love him any longer, but he knew her so well that he would see right away that she was lying. Maybe she should just go back to Mala Kapusta and wait for him to show up so they could talk. But no, she couldn't do that if the fighting had spread to the village. And with fighting in Mala Kapusta, how safe could it be for Alek to go there to leave his letters in the tree trunk?

The more Serafina tried to decide what to do, the more confused she felt and the more worried she became. All the worrying was keeping her up at night, so that she felt listless and tired during the day. When her visitors came, she tried to focus on what they wanted, but it wasn't easy. Then one day a familiar voice called from the gate, and she opened the door to find Dielle waiting for her.

"Dielle!" she cried. "How are you? Come in!"

"I can't stay long," the girl replied. "I heard that you weren't very far away—this is only a few miles from the village where I live—and I wanted to come see you. I had to wait until Mother was well enough to stay home alone."

Dielle stooped to pet Maks before taking a seat at the table. When Dielle was comfortable, Maks began to wind around her legs, purring loudly. "I guess he likes me," she said, reaching down to pet the cat again.

"Yes, he does," Serafina said, surprised. "And he doesn't like many people." Serafina brought out the rest of a loaf that someone had given her the day before and set it on the table along with a soft cheese wrapped in a cloth. After pouring a cup of cider for both of them, she sat down across from Dielle. "How are you doing?"

Dielle gulped half her cider before saying, "Fine, considering that Mother is still weak. But she's in better spirits now, partly because of the duck. I found an orphaned duckling and brought it home and raised it. Mother loves watching it and has taught it to eat from her hand. She even quacks and the duck quacks back. When she carries him, he sticks his head out like this and paddles with his feet as if he's actually swimming." Dielle stretched her neck and made paddling motions with her hands. "I heard her laugh the other day. She hasn't laughed for a very long time. It's good that she has the duck to distract her. That's one of the reasons I'm here, actually. You said you know how to read and write. Do you think you could teach me? That way I could read to Mother and help her think of something other than how sick she feels. I might also be able to make some money writing letters for people or reading out loud the letters they receive."

"I'd be happy to teach you," said Serafina. "I taught my fiancé, Alek."

"I didn't know you had a fiancé. What is he like?"

"Tall, blond, handsome—"

"Tell me more!"

"He's a blacksmith, like his father, and is so strong! He's very kind, too, and is always helping others. I met him when I was six years old. Some bullies were picking on a younger boy in front of my house. Alek made them stop, although the boys hit him, and his mother scolded him for ruining his clothes. He's very sweet, too. He brings me flowers at least once a week. Is there a boy that you like?"

Dielle nodded. "Danya lives down the street. His father makes very fine pottery and Danya's learning to be a potter, too. You've never seen such gorgeous blue eyes! And his voice!" Dielle sighed and had a faraway look in her eyes. "He sang me a song he'd made up once. It was so beautiful!"

"He sounds very nice," said Serafina.

"Oh, he is! Don't tell anyone, but he kissed me behind his father's kiln last week. It was my very first kiss and it was wonderful!"

"Really? When Alek gave me my first kiss, neither of us knew what we were doing. It was nice, but we got much better with practice."

"I like practicing," said Dielle, and both girls laughed.

"Listen!" Serafina said, going to the cupboard. "If you want to learn to read and write, we can start now. I don't know how long I'll be here, but I'll give you a lesson every time you visit. I have an extra quill I can give you. Here's a little pot of ink and some parchment. I'll show you how to write the alphabet and you can practice at home."

"Can you show me how to write my name first? Mother would be so pleased!"

"Of course!" said Serafina. The two girls bent over the parchment until Boris announced that another visitor was at the gate. When Dielle left, Serafina gave her what food she could spare, wishing she had more to give. She was reluctant to see her friend go.

Although Dielle's visit had cheered Serafina, talking about Alek had made her miss him more than ever. Once again she had a restless night and woke the next morning tired and sluggish. She ate her breakfast and went about her morning chores wondering if Dielle would come to see her that day. By midmorning, when she hadn't had any visitors at all, she decided that she couldn't stand being inside for another minute.

Taking the empty firewood basket, Serafina set off for the nearby forest to search for firewood and kindling. She had collected a good supply when she noticed a hole in a tree trunk much like the one in Mala Kapusta where Alek left his notes. A soft sigh escaped her when she thought of Alek. She was startled when a voice spoke to her and a woman only as tall as her shoulder appeared.

"What is wrong, child?" the woman asked.

Serafina expected to answer in her Baba Yaga voice and was astonished when she didn't. Her feelings must have shown on her face because the woman laughed and said, "Don't look so surprised. I asked my first question of a Baba Yaga long ago."

"Who are you?" Serafina asked. The little woman's face was exotic looking, with deep green, slanted eyes and a bow-shaped mouth. Her softly curling hair was a lighter green and hung all the way to the ground, draping across her shoulders and nearly covering her yellow gown.

"I'm the fairy Summer Rose," the woman said. "I've been watching you off and on since the day you became the new Baba Yaga. I wanted to see how you would deal with the responsibility. I thought you were doing very well, considering, but you've seemed distraught lately."

Serafina's heart leaped in her chest. Here was someone who wanted to know how she felt and might actually be able to help her! She felt as if a wall were breaking inside her as all the confusion over Alek poured out in a flood of hopes and fears. She told the fairy about how much she and Alek loved each other, of the plans they'd shared, and how those plans had been dashed the night she went to collect her inheritance. The fairy seemed to know all about the responsibilities of a Baba Yaga and even had some things to tell Serafina.

"There wouldn't be a Baba Yaga if a crazy witch by that name hadn't lied to a fairy long ago. The fairy got so angry that she cursed the witch, making her answer truthfully to the first question anyone asked her. It didn't take long for Baba Yaga to tire of answering questions, especially when she saw how doing so made her grow older and none of her own magic could make her any younger. She dug up skulls and bones to make a fence that would scare people off. When that didn't work, she resorted to killing her visitors. It was her magic that made the skulls talk and stay with her when the cottage moved. She was the cat's first owner and made him talk, too, so he could be her spy."

"She sounds like a dreadful person!" exclaimed Serafina. "What happened to her?"

"She grew older with each question and finally died of old age, a much kinder end than she gave to her victims. The old witch's final cruelty was to pass on the curse to her last visitor, a young woman who had come to ask a question despite the danger."

"So the young woman became the next Baba Yaga?"

"She did, indeed. The witch couldn't end the curse, but she could add to it. She made sure that others would inherit the job. Unlike her, they would all be innocent and pure of heart: the people she hated the most."

"And the blue rose tea?" asked Serafina.

"I took pity on the innocents the witch cursed," said the fairy. "I told the new Baba Yaga that drinking the tea would return her to the age she would have been if the curse hadn't aged her. Each Baba Yaga was supposed to pass the knowledge on to the next, but things have gotten a bit jumbled over the years."

"Were you the fairy the witch lied to—the one who put the curse on her?"

Summer Rose nodded. "I've never been able to abide liars."

"Thank you for telling me all this. The cat doesn't like answering questions, and that book tells me very little."

"The book was just meant to get the new Baba Yaga started. It was never supposed to tell you what to do once you were able to figure things out for yourself. As for the cat, he has a mind of his own. He'll help you only if he wants to, and even then you might not always consider him very helpful. I wish I could help you more, but I'm going away now and I'm not sure when I'll be back." The fairy smiled and patted Serafina's arm. "I just wanted to say that you shouldn't be discouraged and that I think you should see your Alek. Everyone needs a little encouragement now and then."

* * *

Serafina practically flew into the cottage. She'd made up her mind; she'd brew a cup of blue rose tea, drink it, then tell the cottage to return to Mala Kapusta, where she'd wait for Alek to show up even if there was fighting going on. The thought of seeing him again was enough to make her smile. Humming to herself, she put the kettle on to boil and did a little dance step as she carried the clay jar holding the blue rose tea from the cupboard to the table. She was turning to check on the water when she heard Boris shout. Before she could get to the door, it banged open and five men dressed in homespun clothes barged into the cottage, nearly filling the room.

The men moved aside as the roughest-looking one drew closer, almost stepping on Maks, who was standing, back arched and hissing, between him and Serafina.

When the man drew back his foot as if to kick the cat, Serafina scooped up the animal, holding him out of the man's way.

"We're here to get some questions answered," the man snarled, looking down his long, narrow nose at her. Serafina's eyes were drawn to his mouth, where a scar crossed both of his lips. When Serafina didn't say anything, he said in a louder voice, "Answer me, girl. Are you Baba Yaga or not?"

The cat stopped squirming to turn his green-eyed gaze on Serafina's face. "I am Baba Yaga," she answered in her Baba Yaga voice.

"Is it true that you have to answer our questions with the truth?" asked a short man with a bright red burn mark on his face.

"I must answer the first question you ask me with the truth," Serafina said, aware that they'd now wasted two questions.

"What do you mean, the first question?" asked the leader.

"Maybe it means she's not going to answer any others," said the man with the burn.

"I don't need your help," his leader told him, cuffing the back of the shorter man's head. "So tell me," the man said to Serafina. "How can I break into the home of

Master Vasylko Demidas, the richest man in the king-dom, so that I might steal his gold?"

Serafina wasn't surprised that he was a thief or that he would ask such an unsavory question. "Actually, you already asked me a question. I'm not able to answer more than one for each person."

She flinched when he grabbed her arm and shook her. Maks hissed and swiped at the man with his paw, missing only because Serafina jerked him back out of reach.

"I didn't ask you a question yet!" the scarred man shouted in her face.

"Yes, you did," said the shorter man. "You asked her if she was Baba Yaga."

"That doesn't count. It wasn't the question I came here to ask."

"It doesn't matter," Serafina said as she tried to pull away. "Whatever you ask first is the only question I'll be able to answer."

"Really?" said the leader. "I bet you'll tell me with a little persuasion."

Serafina gasped when the man twisted her arm behind her, and pain shot through her shoulder. Maks wiggled in her other arm and she loosened her grip. With a loud yowl, the cat launched himself at the man's face, swiping with his front claws before dropping to the floor.

"Run, Maks!" Serafina shouted as the man let go of her to clap his hands to the long scratches striping both sides of his face. Blood dripped from his cheeks as he tried to grab the cat, who fled out the door.

"I'll kill you and your blasted cat!" the man snarled, pulling a long-bladed knife from its sheath.

He was coming at her with his dagger ready when two of his men stepped between them, blocking his way. "Don't kill her!" said one. "We get questions, too! You kill her and we won't be able to ask them!"

The man glared at his companions as if deciding whether he should kill them as well. Looking frantically around, Serafina was trying to come up with a way to break free when the man shoved his dagger in its sheath. "Ask your questions; then one of you can take care of her," he said, and stomped out the door.

Serafina didn't think that her chances looked very good. There were still four men in the cottage, and she'd already answered a question for the shorter man with the burned face. That meant she would answer three questions, and then they would kill her. She could tell the house to go, but the men would still be in the cottage, unless . . .

The men were arguing with one another, vying to be the first to ask her a question, when she made her way to the bed and sat down. She wished she could warn the cat, but he was outside, probably hiding from the angry man. Two of the thieves were standing by the door when Serafina said in a loud voice, "Chicken hut, chicken hut, take me away from here, and be rough!"

The house stood so quickly that Serafina's stomach felt as if it had plummeted to the ground. She grabbed hold of the bed frame as the cottage tilted from side to side. The two men by the door fell out, screaming, while the other two tumbled to the floor and slid from one side of the room to the other. One man reached for the table leg and had almost gotten a grip on it when the cottage lurched to the other side. He slid across the floor, scrabbling at the floorboards, even as a violent wind carried the skulls through the doorway. They snapped at the man on their way past, and he covered his head with his arms. Unable to stop himself, he flew out the opening, screaming. The man with the burned face was the last thief in the cottage. Despite the floor angling under him, he was able to get to his feet for a moment before the bones clattered through the doorway, hitting him like clubs and shoving him toward the threshold. He fell, thrashing his arms and legs, while the wind flung the yowling cat past him into the cottage.

When the door slammed shut behind the last man, Serafina sat up on the bed. "More gently now, please, house," she called out, and the cottage settled down to its usual amble.

"Clever girl," said Maks, rubbing against her side. He started purring when she scratched him behind the ears.

"I wish I'd thought of it sooner," Serafina told him. "Those were terrible men! And just look at this mess!"

A cup had broken and the pitcher holding fresh wild-flowers lay in shards on the floor. What she found most distressing, however, was that the clay jar that held the blue rose tea was gone. She searched the cottage and eventually found the jar under the bed, but it was empty and the cork was missing.

"Maybe there's more in the cupboard," she muttered to herself as she picked up the empty jar. Though she examined every container on every shelf, she couldn't find any more blue rose tea.

"Do you know where the other Baba Yagas got their tea?" she asked the cat. "Could it have been from the fairy Summer Rose? She said that she was the one who told the first Baba Yaga about it."

"I think it *was* her," he said, yawning. "There used to be a lot of the tea, but that jar held all that was left."

"Oh no!" Serafina said, collapsing onto a chair. "Now I have to find her before I can see Alek! But she said that she was going away. Do you know how to reach her?"

Maks glared at a smudge on his paw as if it had offended him. "I have no idea. No fairy has ever told me her personal business."

"Would the cottage know if I told it to go to her?"

The cat gave his paw a swipe with his tongue before saying, "Hardly! It's lucky it remembers the places it's already been."

"Then I guess I'm going to have to find the roses myself. Maybe they sell them in the market."

"Stranger things have happened," said the cat. "Although it's very unlikely," he added under his breath.

CHAPTER 12

Serafina had never told the cottage to change direction once it had started walking, but she thought it was worth trying. It was in midstride when she said, "Chicken hut, chicken hut, go to a town with a market."

On its next step, the cottage turned just a little but didn't change its pace. It continued walking throughout the day, settling down soon after sunset. Although Serafina couldn't see the town, she could smell smoke from the chimneys and knew that one must be close by.

Early the next morning she put on her second-best gown, collected all her coins, and headed into town. Like Kamien Dom, this town held its market in the central square where two of the larger roads intersected. If

Serafina had looked her real age now, she might have attracted too much attention, but few people spared a glance at the middle-aged woman in ordinary clothes.

It had been so long since she had been away from her cottage that her trip into town was a real treat. She gawked at the peaked roofs and balconies that made this town so different from where she'd grown up and was startled the first time she heard a banner snap in the wind. As she approached the square, she saw vivid red, yellow, blue, and green banners streaming from balcony railings and poles attached to walls. Banners flowed from stalls in the market and from ropes that crisscrossed the air overhead. Serafina even saw smaller versions of the banners woven into girls' hair and wrapped around their waists.

Serafina was in such a good mood that she said hello to everyone who looked her way, not caring that most of the people were being friendly because they saw her as a potential customer. The first farmer she approached was selling onions, garlic, cabbages, and beets from the back of his wagon. His round face was ruddy with a sheen of perspiration from the already-warm day.

"Would you happen to know where I could purchase some blue rose tea?" Serafina asked as she looked over his baskets of produce.

The farmer's friendly smile turned into a smirk. "Do I look like I'm selling tea?"

"No," Serafina said, wishing she could stop herself, but she was already speaking in her Baba Yaga voice. "You look as if you are trying to sell wilted vegetables you picked three days ago and left in the hot sun. You look tired and bored and ready to go home so you can drink the ale you have hidden in the barrel behind the cowshed on your farm. You also look like you're going to steal eggs from your neighbor because your own hens have stopped laying."

"Be quiet!" the red-faced farmer shouted, shooting glances at the older man leaning against the next wagon over.

"What did she say?" the other farmer asked, looking incredulously from Serafina to the first farmer.

Serafina hurried away as the red-faced man denied her allegations. She was making her way through the crowd when she heard a scuffle break out behind her. The crowd thinned as people ran to see who was fighting, leaving Serafina alone in front of a farmer's wife holding a squawking chicken. "Is there something I can do for you?" the sweet-faced woman asked.

"No, there isn't. All I want is blue rose tea and you don't know where I can find it," Serafina said in her

Baba Yaga voice, and was relieved when she didn't say more.

The woman looked thoughtful as she fastened the lid to a crate. "If anyone here knows where to look for a special tea, it would be old Betha. She's down at the end just past the man selling pigs," she said, pointing.

Serafina could see a small pigpen set up near the end of the row, so she thanked the woman and started walking again. When she heard two men talking in low voices, she glanced their way and saw that they were both watching her. She'd never seen the man with the crooked nose before, but the other man looked vaguely familiar. They kept their eyes on her as she walked past; it made her feel uneasy, so she quickened her pace.

Rounding the pen holding squealing piglets, Serafina spotted one last wagon nestled at the base of a brick-and-mortar wall. Bundles of herbs, both fresh and dried, hung from poles above the wagon. A cleared aisle ran down the center with boxes and clay jars crammed together on either side. A little woman who couldn't have been taller than Serafina's chin stood on the wagon bed, her hands on her hips as she watched the crowd below her.

"Are you Betha?" Serafina asked.

"That I am," replied the little woman. "If you're

interested in tea, I have teas that stimulate the appetite, teas that settle the stomach, and teas that aid digestion. I have balm, sage, basil, elderberry flower, catnip, hibiscus, fennel, fenugreek, spicebush, dandelion leaves, rosemary, gentian root, chicory root, angelica, lovage roots, marjoram, savory, peppermint, spearmint, dill—"

"But do you have blue rose tea?" Serafina interrupted.

Betha padded down the aisle to a cluster of small boxes and opened one filled with diced bits of a bright red fruit. "I have rose hip tea. I picked the hips myself last fall, then cut them into pieces and dried them. The tea has a nice tangy flavor."

Serafina felt a spark of hope. This woman might have what she needed! If only the roses were the right color. "And were the roses blue?" she asked.

The little woman reached under her white cap to scratch her head. "I can't say I've ever seen blue roses. No, my rose hips come from dog roses. The blooms are pale pink, not blue."

"Oh," said Serafina. "I need blue rose tea, not pink. Do you know if anyone else might have it?"

The little woman laughed. "If I don't have it, none of the farmers here will. They get their more unusual teas from me. And before you ask if they sell blue roses, I can tell you right now that they don't."

Serafina was disappointed, but she wasn't about to give up. She told herself that being unable to find the tea in one market didn't mean she'd never find it; she'd just have to keep looking.

After thanking Betha, Serafina continued on her circuit of the marketplace. Most of the vendors were selling things they had made, like clay mugs, woven baskets, and leather goods. She was passing a cart where the vendor was selling plates made from a fine, white clay, when the crowd around her shifted, revealing the two men who had been watching her earlier. When she saw that they were still looking in her direction, she began to get nervous. Maybe it was time to go back to the cottage.

Serafina kept an eye on the men and waited until the crowd grew bigger. Slipping behind a large, boisterous family, she started walking. Before she had taken more than a few steps, a hand shot out and grabbed her arm, jerking her to a stop.

"Not so fast!" the man with the crooked nose said, even as he dragged her out of the flow of shoppers. "A friend of ours wants to have a word with you."

The other man bobbed his head up and down. "He's offered a reward and we mean to get it."

"I'm not going anywhere with you!" Serafina told

them, trying to shake off the man's hand. "Help!" she shouted. "Kidnappers!"

A nearby vendor had been talking to a customer, but at the sound of Serafina's voice, he grabbed a cudgel he had hidden under his table and came lumbering toward them. He was a big man who reminded Serafina of Alek and was half again as big as either of her assailants. "Let go of that woman!" he roared. The moment he raised the cudgel above his head, the man with the crooked nose let go of Serafina and took off, his friend right behind him.

"Thank you so much!" Serafina said. She rubbed her arm where the man had held her and shuddered when she thought of what might have happened if the vendor hadn't stepped in.

"Glad I could help," he replied. "No one mistreats a woman when I'm around."

The vendor was returning to his booth when Serafina rejoined the crowd. The two men were nowhere in sight, but she didn't want to take any chances. She kept an eye out for them as she wove her way through the throng, slipping between carts now and then to lose the men if they were following her.

Serafina hurried down the road, thinking that she

might feel safer once she was back in the woods, but when she turned onto the path leading past the cottage, there were so many places for people to hide that her nervousness grew and she began to jump at every little sound. Chiding herself for being silly, she had just come within sight of the cottage when she heard the snap of a twig and a muffled curse. Serafina began to run.

"Open up!" she shouted to Boris, her feet thudding down the path. "Two men are following me!"

Boris swung the gate open with a loud creak, and Serafina dashed into the yard. She had just reached the door when the men came into sight. Darting inside, she slammed the door shut, shouting, "Chicken hut, chicken hut, take me away from here!"

She ran to the window as the floor tilted below her; she'd grown used to walking on an unsteady floor. One of the men was reaching for the gate, but Boris gnashed his teeth, attempting to bite him. The other man had tried to hurdle the fence, but Krany had snapped at him as he'd gone over, snagging the back of his tunic so that he hung, dangling from the skull's grinding teeth. Yure led the rest of the skulls in screaming threats at the men.

Serafina stepped back as the door slammed open, the bones hurtled over the threshold, and the trunk lid flew up. Krany was halfway to the cottage when he let go of the shrieking man, who landed heavily on the ground and curled up in a ball as if that would protect him. Serafina smiled at the skulls as they landed on top of the bones, congratulating themselves on taking care of the men.

"Walk gently, house," she told the cottage, then glanced around the room to see if anything had fallen to the floor and broken. Her gaze landed on the book, lying on the table. Hoping that the book could help her, she took her seat in front of it and opened it to the next blank page. "Where can I find blue rose tea?" she asked.

Serafina held her breath as the page remained blank. Time seemed to stand still as she waited for writing to appear, then suddenly black words crept across the snow-white page, one letter after another.

Blue roses do not exist.

"That's not true," said Serafina. "I know they exist. I drank a cup of blue rose tea!"

If it had been a person who had told her that there were no blue roses, Serafina would have continued to argue, but there was no arguing with a book. Sighing, she closed the cover and pushed the book away. At least she knew now that the book wasn't going to help. She'd just have to find the tea or the fairy Summer Rose without it.

CHAPTER 13

The cottage finally settled at the shady bend of a wide, slow-moving river, not far from a good-sized town. While the front of the cottage faced the road, the back where there were no windows was turned toward the water. Serafina couldn't see the river unless she stepped outside, but she found the constant murmur of the flowing water soothing and walked along its banks whenever she had a few free minutes, hoping to run into a fairy who could tell her how to find Summer Rose.

One day Serafina was standing by the riverbank when she saw a group of riders approaching. Afraid that they might be kidnappers, she didn't want them to catch her away from the cottage, so she watched from a copse of birches, trying to decide if she should go to meet them or hide until they rode off. She was still there when the men dismounted and began to hitch their horses to the trees.

"Don't even think of hitching that beast to my fence!" Boris snapped at a man leading his horse to one of the posts.

Startled, the man jerked back on the bridle. "Did that skull just talk to me?" he asked the men behind him.

Another man stepped forward and Serfina recognized him at once. Toman Damek, the sheriff of Vioska, had come to see her again. While the sheriff told the man where to hitch his horse, Serafina stepped out of the trees and approached her cottage. "Is something wrong, Sheriff Damek?" she asked, meeting him by her gate.

The sheriff nodded toward his men, then opened the gate for Serafina. "I've brought someone to ask you a question," he said. "This man has been trying to convince me of his innocence but has been unable to offer me any real proof. I explained to him that you will answer the first question he asks you with the truth, and that I would believe whatever you say. He has agreed to use his one question now. However, I need to be present to hear your answer, so he can ask you out here if you prefer. His guards will also remain with us."

Serafina glanced back at the men and noticed that all but one were heavily armed. The unarmed man was wearing shackles, and he shuffled to the gate with a guard on either side. "We'll stay out here," she said.

She studied the shackled man as he entered her yard and wondered what he had done. He had a guileless-looking face, and even though he was wearing chains, he walked with his head held high. When she was ready, she looked him in the eyes and said, "Do you understand that you can ask me only one question in your lifetime?" When the man nodded, Serafina said, "What is your question?"

Taking a deep breath, the man said, "Who killed Jeirgif Babin?"

"Laurentij Babin killed his brother and cast the blame on you," Serafina told him, happy to use her Baba Yaga voice. "He has long envied Jeirgif and wants to take over his brother's land and house."

"There!" said the prisoner, stomping his foot. "I told you so! Now do you believe me?"

"I do, indeed," said the sheriff. "You are no longer under arrest, but you must stay under guard until we have arrested Laurentij Babin. If he learns that we have discovered the truth, he might flee the area. Once we have arrested him, you will be set free. If you agree to remain with us until we have returned to Vioska and taken Laurentij Babin into custody, we will release you from your shackles now. Do you agree?"

"Oh yes! Most certainly!" the man cried, relief shining in his eyes.

As the two guards led the man from the yard, Sheriff Damek gave Serafina a small bag. It clinked when he set it in her hand.

"Thank you," he said, bowing his head. "You have been most helpful. The man you just answered is known to be honest, and I did not want him punished for something I felt sure he had not done. The real culprit made a very strong case against him, but I could do nothing without proof. No one will doubt his innocence now."

"You are welcome," Serafina replied. "I'm glad I was able to help an innocent man."

As the group rode away, she wondered how long it would be before the sheriff was back with another request. Somehow, she had no doubt that she would see him again.

Although she was glad she had been able to help Sheriff Damek, she wasn't happy about how much it had made her age. Her eyesight was a bit weaker and her joints had gotten stiffer. Without a way to get young again, Serafina didn't relish answering *any* questions, but it was the only way she could think of that might help her get more of the tea.

A steady stream of people came to see her. Each time she answered a question, she mentioned to her visitor that blue rose tea was what she wanted more than anything. She told so many people that she was sure word had to have gotten around. Although this had worked before when she needed cloth, firewood, or a jug of cider, it didn't seem to do anything now. Scores of people came and went, aging her with each question, but not one of them brought her the tea. Even so, she was reluctant to leave. With so many people knowing that she wanted blue rose tea, the very next visitor might be the one to bring it. Or perhaps the visitor after that.

She considered going to a market town again and looking for the tea herself, but she couldn't stop picturing the faces of the two men who had tried to abduct her. And it wasn't just those two men that she had to worry about. If someone had actually offered a reward for her, others might be looking for her as well. At least in her cottage she felt safe and knew she could get away if necessary.

Serafina had kept the cottage by the bend in the river for nearly four weeks when an old man came to see her. She had seen him stop at the gate before, but this was the first time he had tried to come through.

"Baba Yaga, someone is here to see you!" Boris shouted.

"I can see that," Serafina said from the open doorway. "Won't you come in, sir," she said to her visitor.

The old man glanced up at her through bleary eyes and gave her an appraising look. Appearing satisfied with what he saw, he shuffled forward with his arms held slightly in front of him as if he were being pulled along. Serafina stepped out of his way when he reached the door. "Nice place you got here," he said, peering into the cottage.

"Did you come to ask me a question?"

"I did, indeed," said the old man. "Been putting it off these many days, but I finally asked myself what I was waiting for. If I put it off much longer, either you'll be gone or I will, one way or another."

Taking the seat that Serafina offered, he ran his hand over his bald head, then scratched the fringe of white hair that grew above his ears while Serafina sat down across from him. "You probably have a lot of folks asking you when they're going to die," said the old man. "Well, I don't care about the when or where. It's going to happen someday, and I'd rather it was a surprise.

Nope, what I want to know isn't about me at all. My question is about my family. What's going to happen to them after I'm gone?"

"You have three fine children, and they are all going to prosper," Serafina said, hearing her voice change. "Your older son is well respected and liked. He will be mayor of your town someday. Your daughter will have eight children who will grow up healthy and strong. Your younger son will sail the seven seas. One day his ship will founder off the coast of a tropical island. He'll make it to shore, where he'll meet a beautiful native girl. They'll marry and have eleven children, nine of them boys."

The old man nodded. "My older son is already loved and respected in town. He's the kind of man that people look up to. My daughter has three children now. So she's going to have five more? Who would have thought it! I'm not surprised about my youngest. He's gotten into more scrapes than I can count and gotten out of them on his own just fine every time. Still, it's good to know."

Sitting back in the chair, he steepled his fingers over his comfortable paunch and smiled. "That takes care of them, but now I have another question for you."

"I'm afraid I can answer only one question for each person," Serafina told him.

"Baba Yaga can answer only one question, but I'm not asking her. I'm asking you, the woman who speaks like a normal person. You're a fine figure of a woman and seem to be around my age. My wife died a few years ago, and my children moved out long before that. I have plenty of money and a big house that I'm tired of rattling around in all by myself. My friends are always trying to match me up with their young daughters who wouldn't mind marrying a rich old man who's bound to die soon, but I'd rather marry a gal my own age who won't be waiting for me to kick the bucket. I know we just met, but you're the sort of woman I've been looking for."

"Someone who lives in a house that walks around on chicken legs?" asked Serafina.

"Haw!" the old man barked, slapping his knee. "I knew I'd like you! So what do you say?"

"I find your offer very flattering, but I'm going to have to decline," said Serafina. "I'm not the age you think I am, nor am I available. I've already promised my hand to someone."

The old man ran his fingers over his bald scalp again. "Doesn't that just figure! Well, it doesn't hurt to ask, now, does it? And feel free to reconsider. You can even take a few days to think about it. Oh, before I forget, here's the gift I owe you." Reaching into his pocket, he handed her a small carved wooden box. "It's a neck-lace that belonged to my wife. Thank you for my answer."

"And thank you for your gift. But if this was your wife's, you should give it to your daughter." She pressed the box into his hand.

The old man looked distressed. "I can't take this back! I have to give you something!"

"Then you can answer a question for me," said Sera-fina. "I've let it be known that I would like some blue rose tea, yet no one has brought me that particular gift. Do you have any idea why that is?"

"Can't say as I do," the old man said, shaking his head. "But I can find out. Blue rose tea, you say? I'll get back to you as soon as I can."

* * *

Dielle appeared on her doorstep early the next day, look-ing tired and more ragged than she had before. "Are you all right?" Serafina asked, pulling her inside.

Dielle dropped onto a chair. Crossing her arms on the table, she rested her head on them. "I didn't get much sleep last night. Mother was really restless. This morn-ing a neighbor told me that you were out this way, so I came by to see how you were doing." Lifting her head from her arms, she turned toward Serafina. "You looked so old last time, and you look even older now. When I told my mother how you get old when you answer questions, she said I should have offered to help you. Can I do anything for you? Sweep the floor or burn your trash or fetch water? Just name it and I'll do it while I'm here."

"Thank you, but no," said Serafina. "I am older, but I can still do what I need to. It just takes me longer now."

"I heard that you're looking for something."

"I'm looking for blue rose tea, but no one seems to have any. I've looked everywhere and haven't been able to find it, so now I'm asking people to look for me."

"I can look, too, you know. Why didn't you ask me?"

"I would have, but I didn't know I needed it until after your last visit. It's the only thing that makes my body young again. The problem is, all the blue rose tea I had is gone, and without it I'm going to keep getting older until I die. Don't worry," Serafina said when Dielle scowled. "I have enough people looking for the tea that I'm sure someone will find it. Tell me, how is your writing going? Have you been practicing?"

Dielle smiled and sat back in her seat. "Every day! If you have a piece of parchment, I can show you. I covered every bit of the one you gave me, and I think I can make the letters pretty well now."

"I have some parchment right here," Serafina said, going to the cupboard. "I've told people that I need it and have been given quite a lot. Here, let me see what you can do."

Serafina sat down to watch Dielle write the alphabet slowly and carefully. She was delighted that her friend didn't need any prompting. "Good!" said Serafina when Dielle lay down her quill. "Now we'll practice the sounds and putting letters together."

They worked for nearly an hour before Serafina got up to get them something to eat. Dielle was reaching for another piece of cold sausage when she said, "Does everyone in your family read and write?"

"Just my father and me. My sisters and my mother weren't interested in learning."

"How many sisters do you have?"

"Two and they're both older than me."

"Are they married?"

Serafina nodded. "Alina is married to a nice man named Yevhen. They just had a baby boy. They named him Osip. My older sister is Katya. She's married to Viktor."

Dielle swallowed a bite of bread to ask, "Is he nice, too?"

Serafina laughed. "'Nice' is the last thing I'd call

Viktor. My great-aunt got me to come to this cottage by telling me that I would receive an inheritance. Viktor was the one who brought me, and on the way he said that he wanted a share of whatever I got. I was mad then, but now I wish I could give him all of it! Imagine, an oaf like Viktor being Baba Yaga!"

"Do you really hate being Baba Yaga so much?" asked Dielle.

Serafina thought for a moment before answering. "Sometimes I do and sometimes I don't. I hate getting older without being able to do anything about it, and I hate not seeing my family and friends. I especially hate not being with Alek. But there are a lot of things that I actually enjoy, like Maks and the skulls and meeting all kinds of people and seeing new places."

"And being able to see fairies!"

"And that, too," Serafina said with a smile. "I also love that I've been able to make a new friend."

"So do I! Although your new friend is going to eat all your sausage," Dielle said, reaching for the plate.

"Go right ahead," Serafina told her, pushing the plate toward her. "I can always ask for more!"

"Would it be all right if I took some of this back to Mother?" Dielle asked, her hand hovering over the sausage.

"Good idea!" said Serafina. "And someone brought me a sack of potatoes that you can have, too."

The girls raided the cupboard, although Dielle was careful not to take too much. "The way things are going, people might not be able to keep you so well supplied."

"But there's only one of me and two of you," Serafina replied.

"*Mrowr!*" said Maks.

Serafina chuckled. "I stand corrected! There are two living here as well!"

When the sack of food was ready, Dielle gave Serafina a hug. "I should go now if I'm to get home before dark. Thank you again for being so kind to us. Mother and I really do appreciate it."

"You're welcome," Serafina said, returning the hug. "Please say hello to her for me. Oh, wait! There's one other thing." Leaving Dielle at the door, Serafina returned to the cupboard and took out a small book that a visitor had given to her. "Here, take this, too. You can practice your reading. Bring it with you the next time you come and we'll go over it together."

"Thank you so much!" Dielle said, her eyes shining.

"You're welcome!" said Serafina, and she gave her one more hug. "Safe travels!"

Serafina stood at the door, waving until Dielle was out of sight. She enjoyed her friend's visits tremendously, partly because she really liked her company and partly because her visits made life seem almost normal. Going back into the cottage, Serafina closed the door behind her, wondering when she might see her friend again.

* * *

The next night, Serafina was getting ready for bed when she heard Boris shout, "You have company!"

"Who could it be at this hour?" Serafina murmured as she refastened her gown. She had been busy all day, receiving one visitor after the other; all she wanted to do was go to sleep. Pulling her shawl around her shoulders, she opened the door and peered outside. Three figures were standing by the gate, and she could hear others on horseback in the gloom under the trees.

"Which one of you has a question for me?" she called, trying to see their faces in the dark. Her eyes weren't very sharp anymore, and she couldn't tell if they were men or women, young or old.

"I do," one of the figures said in a young man's voice, stepping forward.

"Then you may enter, but the others must stay

beyond the gate," she told him, and turned back to take her seat at the table.

She was sitting down when her visitor stepped into the candlelight and she could finally see his face. He was a sturdy young man with a thick-set body, dark hair, and darker eyes; she could see right away that he bore a strong resemblance to King Borysko. "I'm Prince Cynrik of Vargas," he told her. "You've spoken with my father."

"I remember. It was one of my more memorable visits," said Serafina. "Please sit down. You'll give me a crick in my neck if I have to look up at you like this."

"My father told me about you," Prince Cynrik said, taking a seat, "but you're a lot older than the woman he described."

Serafina gave him a wry smile. "My age is known to vary from day to day."

"Uh-huh," he said, sounding skeptical. "I don't know how that's possible, but I have heard that your predictions are very accurate."

"I don't make predictions. I simply answer questions with the truth. One question for each person over an entire lifetime, so be careful what you ask."

"I know exactly what I want to ask. My question is—what can I do to end the war?"

Serafina turned her head away. When she'd first seen his face, she'd had a good idea what he was going to ask, but she hated giving answers that might lead to someone's death. All she could do was hope that she was about to tell him something that would bring a quick end to the war. And then her mouth opened without her control, and she said in Baba Yaga's voice, "First you must rid yourself of the traitors in your midst. Lord Dymtrus, Lord Jerrel, and Lord Vanko have all been lining their pockets with gold from Lord Zivon, a supporter of your father's enemy, King Kolenka. In exchange for the gold, the three lords have been informing Zivon of your father's plans. Rid your father's court of these men and replace them with three of his staunchest supporters, Lord Dima, Lord Lyaksandro, and Lord Rufin. Three days before the new moon, send a small fleet to the Daleko Strait. Let King Kolenka's men pursue them to the Isle of Ptaks. Keep the rest of your fleet hidden behind the isle and prepared to fall on Kolenka's navy once it has rounded the promontory . . ."

Serafina continued to tell the prince exactly what to do, outlining where he should send his forces and what places to avoid. "And whatever you do," she said finally, "don't join in the battles yourself. You are a strong and valiant warrior, but you will be killed if you fight. Peace will follow if you live; chaos will reign if you do not."

"I understand," said Prince Cynrik as he rose to his feet. "But how do I know that this isn't a trick? If I do what you say and you're actually helping Zivon or Kolenka, I'll be handing the victory over to them."

"Hey, you came to me!" Serafina said in her own voice. "I answered your question with the truth. It's up to you to decide what to do with it."

The prince searched her eyes with his as if to hunt out any hint of deception. Finally, he seemed to come to a decision; he nodded and reached for a small leather bag hanging from his belt. "Here is your gift," he said, laying it on the table. "My father trusted your word and so shall I. I'm sorry if I was rude, but it is hard to trust anyone in times like this."

"I know," Serafina said, thinking of the man who had offered a reward for her.

"I'll have to trust you with one other thing—that you won't tell anyone what you told me," he said, a question in his eyes.

Serafina straightened her bent back as much as she could, a difficult task as she'd aged even more in the last few minutes. "I would never repeat what I told you to anyone of my own free will. However, a Baba Yaga has

166

no control over what she says when asked a first question."

"I cannot ask for anything more," said the prince. "I see what you mean about aging. You look older now than when I came in."

"I know," she said, examining one of her age-spotted hands.

"You said 'a Baba Yaga.' Does that mean there's more than one?"

Serafina shook her head. "There's only one at a time." Blowing out the candle on the table, she started toward the door, hoping the prince would take the hint. She was so tired that her bones ached, and she wanted to go to bed.

After thanking her again, Prince Cynrik finally left. The door was hardly shut behind him when Serafina retrieved the mirror from the cupboard. Standing in front of the candle she'd left burning on the mantel, she peered at her reflection. She looked almost as ancient as her old neighbor, Widow Zloto. Soft wrinkles creased her face, and tiny lines radiated from the outside corners of her eyes. Her hair was nearly all white, and the backs of her hands were dotted with age spots. A silent sob caught in her throat when she thought of what Alek might say if he saw her now. He would be kind and gentle and say all the right things, but even he would know that they could never be together or have a family. He would pity her, too, and that was something she would not be able to stand.

Setting the mirror on the table, she blew out the candle and shuffled to her bed, her footsteps slow and hesitant. Maks was curled up near her pillow, but he moved over when she lay down and pulled up the covers. When her body shook with silent tears, he shifted closer to snuggle against her back. Neither of them said a word, but she was grateful for the comfort and warmth of his body.

Serafina would have told the cottage to leave that night, but first she wanted to talk to the old man who had promised to find the answer to her question about the blue rose tea. Afraid of how much she would age if she answered any more questions, she told Boris not to let anyone in but the old man with the bald head who had come before. The skull took his job seriously, shouting at everyone else to go away. Each time she heard Boris's voice, Serafina peeked through the window to see who was there. Then one day another man arrived; it was someone she felt she couldn't turn away.

Once again the sheriff's armed guard was escorting a shackled man. Serafina watched through the window as they tethered their horses. The prisoner came to the gate seeming more interested than apprehensive, which made Serafina think he might be as innocent as the last man the sheriff had brought.

When Serafina stepped outside, Boris was already shouting, "Go away! Baba Yaga doesn't want to see anyone now."

"Wait, Boris! I'll make an exception for Sheriff Toman Damek," she said, watching the prisoner's face. He had appeared startled when he heard the skull and saw the jaws moving, but his look of astonishment quickly turned into a smirk. Serafina didn't like his expression, nor did she like it when he turned his head to spit at her gate. This was one man she would never have let in her cottage.

"Your prisoner can ask his question out here," she told the sheriff, who nodded and gestured for his men to bring the prisoner inside the fence.

"Do you know you may ask only one question of me your entire life?" she said once the prisoner stood before her.

The man's smirk grew broader. "I don't know why I'd ever want to ask you anything, old woman. Baba Yaga is just a myth. There is no such person any more than there are fairies or trolls. You're profiting from people's ignorance by pretending to answer their questions."

"Be polite!" ordered the sheriff.

Serafina shrugged. "Think what you will, I'll answer your question regardless. What is it you wanted to ask me?"

"I'm not asking—"

"Ask her the question," one of the guards said, prodding him from behind. "You know that's why we came here."

The prisoner shrugged and said in an insolent voice, "I won't believe a word she says. I know it's going to be all lies, and anyone who does believe her is an idiot and a fool. If I'd stolen those sheep, where are they now? You've been to my farm, sheriff. You've seen that I have no sheep to my name. And what about the money? You tore my house apart, claiming I might have sold them, even though I swore that I have no more money than I've ever had. But I'll ask her your question because you say that I'll hang for sure if I don't."

"Ask her!" said Sheriff Damek.

"I know, I know!" the man spit at the sheriff. Turning back to Serafina, he growled, "Did I steal the sheep from the common land in Vioska?"

Serafina looked him in the eyes when she answered

in her Baba Yaga voice. "You stole the sheep from the common land three weeks ago. Two weeks before that you stole the sheep from the farms belonging to Matviyko Klimus and his neighbor Svec Ruza. Both times you sold the sheep to Mlynar Leva, a dealer in Istina, then gave the money to Lord Zivon, the man you've been working for all along. He has been giving the money to King Kolenka, which means you are a traitor to your king as well as a thief and a liar."

The prisoner's eyes had grown round and large while Serafina spoke. He began spluttering before she was finished. "No! That's not true! I told you she would lie! I'd never—"

"Take him back to his horse and tie him on so he can't move," the sheriff told his men. "You heard the answer. This is a matter for the king now. I'll send two men back with word for the new sheriff, and the rest of you will be going with me to take him before the king himself."

The prisoner was blubbering when the men dragged him through the gate. He looked so terrified that Serafina almost felt sorry for him.

"Once again I owe you my thanks," the sheriff told her. "I would not have brought him to you if he had simply been a thief, but I was sure there was more to it and I was right."

"I'm glad I was able to help," said Serafina. "So tell me, should I expect this to become a regular event—you bringing prisoners to me so I can prove their guilt or innocence?"

Sheriff Damek shook his head. "That won't be likely. After today, I'm no longer sheriff of Vioska. I've received word that I'm needed at the king's side. When I leave here, I'm going straight to the castle. I wanted to take care of this one last matter before I let my successor take over, because I suspected the very thing you told the prisoner. Now I have names I can pass on to King Borysko and a better chance that we can catch the culprits."

"Then I wish you well," Serafina said as he handed her a small bag of coins.

"Wow!" said Boris, watching the sheriff and his men ride away. "I really enjoyed that."

"I knew that man was guilty as soon as I aimed my eye sockets at him," Krany announced. "Anyone with eyes that green can't be telling the truth."

"The prisoner didn't have green eyes," said Serafina. "That was the sheriff."

"I always said that Krany doesn't know what he's talking about!" Yure chortled.

* * *

The old man arrived two days later. Before she'd even peeked outside, Serafina knew from the welcoming tone of Boris's voice that the old man was there. She was always cold now, so she pulled her shawl tighter around her thin shoulders and opened the door, beckoning her visitor in with a wave of her hand.

The old man looked at her oddly when he stepped inside, but he seemed happy enough to take a seat at her table. "I looked into that question you wanted answered," he said. "The reason no one has brought you blue rose tea is because no one knows where to find it. A lot of people seem to think that you give better answers if the gift is something you want, so believe me when I say that when you ask for something, people try to bring it to you. They've been looking for it everywhere without any luck."

Serafina thought about telling the old man that she had no control over the answers she gave and that the gift was more a courtesy than a payment, but she didn't think she wanted everyone to know that. She depended on the gifts, and the more she thought about it, the more she thought they really were payments of a sort. If Baba Yaga didn't receive something when she answered questions, she might avoid people so she wouldn't age, an idea that Serafina found very appealing.

She realized now how much her hopes had been tied to the old man's answer. She'd thought someone might have seen blue roses in a faraway market, or someone might have known someone else whose cousin had them growing in her garden. Hearing him say that no one knew anything about them made her hope melt like a patch of ice on a warm day. Without the tea, her ever-aging body would probably die of old age before the fairy Summer Rose returned.

"Thank you for asking around," she said, her heart so heavy that she found it difficult to breathe.

The old man shrugged. "I'm sorry I couldn't be more helpful."

Serafina glanced toward the window, wondering how soon she could tell the house to leave, then turned back to the old man when he suddenly leaned toward her, squinting.

"What's wrong?" she asked, his close scrutiny making her uncomfortable.

"My eyes must be failing me," he replied. "You look a lot older than I thought you did the other day. I could have sworn that you were my age, but now . . . How old are you, if you don't mind my asking?"

Serafina struggled to her feet, her mind made up. "I'm a lot younger than I look."

"Well, you look a lot older than me. About that proposal . . ."

"Don't worry," she told him, taking him by the elbow so she could hustle him to the door. "I don't plan to marry you. If I were you, I'd hurry home. It's time I was on my way, and you don't want to be in my yard when I leave."

Although Serafina usually preferred to wait until dark to tell the cottage to move, this time she couldn't bring herself to wait that long. The most she could do was watch through the window until the old man was out of sight before calling in Maks and taking a few items from the cupboard. She was sitting at the table when she told the cottage, "Chicken hut, chicken hut, take me to Mala Kapusta and walk gently. My body is getting too frail for this kind of thing."

Maks braced himself as the cottage stood. When the floor was fairly level again, he strolled to Serafina's side and rubbed against her leg, purring. She didn't respond, so he jumped onto her lap and nudged her arm with his head. "What are you doing?" he asked.

"Something I should have done long before this." Scowling at a teardrop on the parchment, she thought about what she wanted to say. It took her nearly an hour to write the letter, and the cat stayed in her lap purring the entire time. When Serafina finally finished the note, she sat back to read it while the ink dried.

Dear Alek,

You mean so much to me, but I can't share your hope and expectations. We aren't meant to be together. I have run out of the blue rose tea that keeps me young and can't find any more. My body has aged so much that I can't have long to live. I love you and always will, but do not look for me. Go live your life without me. I'm sure you will meet someone else to love someday.

Love,
Fina

There were so many other things that Serafina had wanted to say, yet she couldn't bring herself to say them. She wanted to tell Alek that she was devastated, that she would love him forever, that she really didn't want him to find someone else to love but because she loved him she wanted him to be happy, even if it meant he would love someone else. Her tears were flowing freely when she finished the letter, but she was careful to keep them from falling on the parchment.

It was midafternoon when the cottage reached Mala

Kapusta, but Serafina didn't care who saw her. Before the cottage had finished settling to the ground, she told the skulls and bones not to bother making the fence because they wouldn't be there long, but they didn't listen and flew out the door, forming the fence even as she hurried across the road. Two letters and a fresh bouquet were waiting for her in the hole in the tree. One letter was from Alek, the other from her father. After shoving her own letter into the hole, she made her way back across the road and climbed onto her bed to let herself have a good cry. "Chicken hut, chicken hut, take me somewhere far from any towns or villages," she told the cottage. She didn't bother to tell it to be gentle.

A few hours later, with her tears dried and her curiosity growing stronger, she finally opened the letter from her father.

> *My darling daughter,*
>
> *I'm writing to you because Alek says he has a way to get letters to you. He has also told us what happened to you. Your mother thinks her grandmother really did have a sister named Sylanna, but we are still angry that we were deceived like that. To think that a member of our own family would trick us about an inheritance!*

As for Viktor, everyone was furious when we learned that he let you go into the cottage alone. Your mother hasn't spoken to him since.

We worry about you, but Alek assures us that you are well. The widow Zloto comes by every day to ask if we've had any word of you. Your mother thinks we should invite her to move in, she is here so often. I don't know if I could survive that much chatter!

Ah—our big news! Three days after you left for Mala Kapusta, your sister Alina gave birth to a healthy baby boy. We were thrilled, although our joy would have been greater if you had been here with us to welcome him to our family. Your mother and I think he looks like Alina did as a baby, but Widow Zloto insists he looks like her brother-in-law did when he turned ninety-five.

Everything is going well with my work. I have a new apprentice, but he is clumsy and has fallen off a ladder twice. Perhaps I should help him find a safer career that does not involve ladders.

Your mother and I worry about you day and night, but especially about your travels through Vargas while it is at war with Khrebek. Alek is

178

also worried and has been trying to find a way to free you of being Baba Yaga. I do what I can to help him, although I am no longer a young man. Be assured that none of us will rest until we have brought you home again.

> *Love,*
> *Your father*

The other letter was from Alek.

Fina,

I thought it might help keep your spirits up to hear the news from home, so here it is. I finished the sword and even my father says it is the best work I have ever done. Now Sir Ganya wants me to make another just like it as a gift for his brother.

I think you'll be interested to hear that my father is suddenly the most eligible bachelor in town. Since my mother's death, Father hasn't looked at another woman. That does not mean that they have not been looking at him. Now, after three years, they all seem to think that he is fair game. The butcher's sister has been bringing Father fine cuts of meat. The tailor's twin daughters have both been after him. One mends his clothes, the other stops by to clean our house. Now the niece of the owner of the Roaring Lion tavern is bringing him hot meals. When he stops in at the tavern, she gives him free ale. I asked Father which woman he likes the best, but he said he cannot choose. Separately, they are taking very good care of him, but if he proposes to one, he will disappoint the rest and not have such a fine life!

I miss you, Serafina. Every time I see something interesting or think of something funny, I want to run to your house to tell you about it. Although that cannot happen now, someday we will be together, I am sure of it.

Before the war started, I traveled through Vargas to learn what I could about freeing you of the Baba Yaga curse. Although I did not learn anything of value, I did not give up. Lately I have been talking to people who have come to Pazurskie for refuge from the war. Many do not even believe in Baba Yaga, but there are also many who talk freely about you. I still hope to meet someone who can tell me what I need to know.

I understand that you travel from place to place throughout the region. Be careful, sweet one. I hate

that we are apart, but I hate even more that you
spend any time at all in a kingdom that is at war.

Love,
Alek

Clutching both letters to her chest, Serafina lay down on her bed and let the rocking motion of the walking cottage lull her to sleep.

CHAPTER 14

Serafina stood in her doorway, looking out across the endless progression of rolling waves. The cottage had brought her to the top of a seaside cliff just the day before, and she could envision herself staying there for a very long time. Although she had no idea what kingdom she might be in, it seemed that the cottage stayed mostly in Vargas. She doubted she'd meet anyone here, however. As far as she could tell, there were no villages or towns nearby, and the only ships she'd spotted had been too far out on the water for her to see clearly. She thought it was perfect.

Maks brushed past her on his way out the door. "I'm going to look around. Maybe I'll find a nice crisp grasshopper for breakfast."

"Don't get lost," said Serafina.

The cat made a delicate coughing sound. "I never have!" he said, and scampered off between the bones of the fence into the tall grass beyond.

"I think I'll go for a walk, too," Serafina said to herself, and went inside to retrieve her shawl. A few minutes later she was back and ready for Boris to open the gate.

"Stay close by," he said. "You never know what you'll find in wild places like this."

"There isn't even a road, Boris," Serafina replied. "I don't think we'll see any people here."

"It wasn't people I was talking about," the skull muttered, swinging the gate closed behind her.

"He means ogres and trolls and . . . ," Yure began.

"I'm sure she knows what I mean," Boris told him.

Yure's jaws closed with a snap.

Good, thought Serafina. *If ogres and trolls live here, maybe fairies do, too. This could be where Summer Rose came. I might be able to find her yet!*

Serafina glanced from side to side as she tried to decide where to explore. To the left of the cottage, the tall grass continued until the land dropped out of sight about two hundred yards away. To the right, wind-stilted trees grew all the way to the cliff's edge, but a glint of water farther back among the trees caught her eye. She would go that direction first.

The wind was stronger than Serafina had expected, buffeting her as she walked to the woods. She was relieved when she finally reached the shelter of the trees. It didn't take her long to find the water—a stream that switched back and forth through the forest until it plunged over the edge of the cliff. Upthrust rocks formed a partial barrier on one side, cutting down on the wind even more. Although she could still hear the ocean, the sound was muted and the wind was no more than a gentle breeze. Closing her eyes, she took a deep breath, enjoying the smells of the forest and the salty tang of the ocean.

"I like the way it smells, too," said a deep, rumbly voice.

Serafina looked around, but all she could see were the trees and rocks. Then something that she'd thought was a boulder shifted. Serafina gawked in astonishment when she realized that it wasn't a boulder but an exceptionally large man.

"Please, sit down and join me," he said, gesturing to the rock where he'd been perched. "It's been so long since I've had someone to talk to."

Serafina hadn't expected to see anyone in the woods.

184

If she had known that there was anyone nearby, she would have stayed in her cottage or even had the cottage move again. The last thing she wanted to do was answer another question and grow even older. She looked as stunned as a deer caught in the firelight that was poised to take off if only she could look away.

The big man chuckled. "Don't worry, I'm not going to ask you any questions."

"Then you know who I am," said Serafina.

"Of course. I saw the chicken footprints and followed them here. When they led me to a house instead of an enormous chicken, I knew that I'd found Baba Yaga."

Serafina was torn. She was still afraid that he would ask her something, even if he didn't mean to, but then again it would be nice to have someone to talk to who didn't expect anything from her. Curiosity finally made her ask, "Are you a giant?"

"I am, indeed," he said, looking serious. "I'm the very last of my kind."

"That explains why you're lonely," Serafina said, half to herself.

The giant nodded. "I've been alone for five years, and they've been the longest years of my life."

"What happened to the other giants?" she asked.

The giant didn't seem to mind her question. He

shrugged, and it was like a hilltop moving. "I went away for a few years, and when I came back, all of my family and friends were gone."

Without realizing it, Serafina had drifted closer to the giant until she was only a few yards away. She was near enough now to estimate his height; he had to be at least twelve feet tall. "If I sit down, will you sit down, too? You're too tall to talk to if you don't."

"It would be my pleasure," he replied.

She glanced at the boulder that he'd been using as a seat. It was chest high, far too high for her to climb onto.

"Here, let me help you," said the giant. He set his hands gently on her waist, his enormous fingers overlapping, and picked her up as easily as if she were a tiny bird. Then he placed her on the boulder, and she sat, dangling her legs over the side, while he lowered himself to the ground beside her.

Even though the giant was sitting, Serafina felt like a tiny child in the company of an adult. His head was more than twice as big as hers, each eye as large as a goose egg. The thought popped into her head that she wouldn't want to be around when he blew his nose, and she had to stifle a fit of giggles by pretending to cough.

"We don't have to talk if you don't want to," said the

giant. "I just like having you here. My name is Auster, by the way."

"I'm Serafina," she told him. "You don't happen to know if there are any fairies in the neighborhood, do you? I'm looking for one named Summer Rose."

The giant shook his head. "Sorry, there could be dozens right around here and I'd never know it. Fairies tend to avoid giants; I guess because we're so clumsy and they're so easily crushed."

They talked about the weather then, and how much they liked the forest. Serafina quickly realized how easy it was to talk to Auster, and they were soon chatting as companionably as if they were old friends. She told him about her family and how confused and upset they had sounded in the letter she had received from her father. When she mentioned Alek and how she'd decided that she should never see him again, she couldn't keep the tears from trickling down her cheeks. Auster told her about his family and friends and how he felt when he came home and found them gone. He had spent the last five years looking for them and had only just decided that they were gone forever. When she saw how sad he looked, she turned the conversation to other things, like the interesting people they'd met and places they'd seen.

It was nearly dark when Serafina finally asked

Auster to help her get down from the rock. Once on her feet, she swayed slightly and he reached out to steady her, then broke off a sturdy branch and fashioned it into a cane that she could use to get home. They said goodbye, and though neither one mentioned seeing each other again, Serafina was sure that they would.

They fell into a regular routine after that. Serafina would eat a simple breakfast, then go for a walk in the woods. The giant was always there when she arrived. Sometimes they would have long conversations, and other times they would sit in comfortable silence. Sometimes they would stay in the forest, while other times they went for a walk along the cliff, although Serafina's fear of heights made her stay away from the edge. At least once a day, Auster would say how much he missed his family and friends. Serafina tried not to mention Alek because it hurt so much to think of him.

One day they were sitting at the edge of the woods, looking out to sea, when Auster stood up and stared into the distance, using his hand to shade his eyes from the sun.

"What is it?" asked Serafina.

"Ships," he said. "Over there!"

Serafina looked where the giant was pointing and could just make out some dark, tiny specks. As she watched, the specks grew bigger, until she could see that they were indeed ships. Within moments more specks came into view behind them.

Auster watched as intently as she did when the ships crossed in front of them, too far out to see the devices on their flags or the people manning the ships. It soon became clear that the second and larger set of ships was pursuing the first. Serafina wondered if the ships belonged to King Borysko and his enemy, King Kolenka, but from such a distance she had no way of knowing. For the first time since she'd arrived at the cliff, she wondered what was happening in the world she'd left behind and what exactly she was missing.

Serafina met with Auster again the next day, but this time she was unable to enjoy their conversation. She'd begun to feel as if there was something she should be doing and she was wasting her time by not doing it. Auster didn't say anything, but he gave her more than one searching look and didn't act surprised when she wanted to return to her cottage early.

Seeing the ships had made Serafina remember King Borysko's war. Was Alek all right? What if he got caught up in the fighting? What if the fighting spread to Pazurskie and Kamien Dom?

She was on her way back to the cottage, her mind

awhirl with all the awful possibilities, when she heard someone sobbing. The sound was so heart-wrenching that Serafina couldn't help but go see who was crying. Following the sound through the trees, she came across a young woman with pale green skin and long, fluttery hair bent over and crying as if she was in pain.

"What's wrong?" Serafina asked.

The girl took her hands from her face to peer at Serafina through her tears. "This awful dust has settled on my saplings! Just look at what it's doing to my leaves!" she said, jumping to her feet.

Serafina blinked. The girl's dilemma wasn't at all what she'd expected, but then the girl was unusual as well. As Serafina drew closer, she noticed that the girl smelled like the trees themselves and had a strange grainy texture to her skin. It occurred to her that this was a nymph who lived in and with the trees. Of course she would be upset if her trees were ailing! Serafina had never met a nymph before, but then she had never met a giant, either.

The girl brushed her finger along one of the yellow, drooping leaves. A puff of white dust rose around the leaf, then settled back onto it. "This dust is evil! What can I do to help my trees?"

Resigned to answering another question—the last thing she wanted to do—Serafina said in her Baba Yaga voice, "That isn't dust. Those are tiny white flies that are sucking the life from your trees. Contact the frost fairy. She can use her ice selectively to freeze the flies and kill them."

"Really? How wonderful! Thank you for telling me!" said the nymph as she turned to leave.

"Before you go," said Serafina, "do you know where I can find the fairy Summer Rose?"

"I have no idea," the green-skinned girl said, shaking her head. "I don't think I've ever met a fairy by that name. Sorry!"

Serafina sighed as she watched the nymph slip into the forest. For the briefest moment she had hoped that her problem might be solved. *Ah well*, she thought. *At least I was able to help someone.*

Serafina was surprised that she felt so good about what she'd done. She had seen how happy she had made the nymph with her answer, as if she had averted a terrible tragedy. It was a satisfying feeling and it lightened her gloomy mood. It also made her start thinking about just why she was hiding from people and their endless questions. True, answering questions as Baba Yaga made her body age and she no longer had any way to reverse it, but she knew that the blue rose tea did exist, even if it was extraordinarily hard to find. If she continued to look, she was sure she'd be able to find either the tea or Summer Rose someday. And what good was a Baba Yaga if she didn't answer people's questions and help them at difficult times? While she might not be able to help everyone, at least she could give some real assistance to some of the people some of the time, which was more than most people could claim. By the time she closed her eyes in bed that night, Serafina knew what she had to do. She would return to civilization, but only after she had spoken with Auster.

The giant looked mournful when she found him sitting on the boulder the next morning. "I can sense that something in you has changed," he said. "You're leaving today."

Serafina nodded. "I am. And so are you. I've never said this before, but I want you to ask me a question. It should be about something that really matters to you. Maybe something that you've been thinking about for the last five years."

Auster looked confused at first, but then his eyes lit up and he straightened his back from his dejected

192

slouch. "I hadn't thought of that! I know about the Baba Yaga's ability to tell the truth, but it never occurred to me to come to you for help. All right, then. Where did all my family and friends go?"

"Fifteen years ago the leader of the giants learned of a new kingdom where land was plentiful and humans were sparse," Serafina said in her Baba Yaga voice. "He convinced the Council of Giants to build ships that could carry them all due west across the sea to their future home. Family after family set sail. Though your family waited for you, even they could wait for only so long. You were away on your errand for two years. They had already been gone a year when you returned."

"Due west, you say?" Auster replied. "How many days' sailing?"

"I have no idea," Serafina said in her own voice.

"Sorry, I forgot: one question only. I guess I need to build my own ship, which should be interesting. I've never built a ship before. I know! I'll get the gnomes to help. They'll build anything for gold, and I have plenty of that. I don't know how to thank *you*, though."

"You were my friend when I needed one," Serafina told him. "I'm just glad I was able to help you."

"But isn't there anything you need that I could give you?"

"There is one thing," said Serafina. "You don't happen to know where I can find some blue roses, do you?"

Auster shook his head. "I've seen plenty of roses, but none of them were blue."

"It never hurts to ask," said Serafina.

CHAPTER 15

Soon after Serafina arrived in the forest where she'd met Dielle, her friend stopped by. "Where have you been?" she asked as Serafina opened the door.

Serafina stepped aside as Dielle strode past to set a small basket filled with fresh-picked berries on the table. "I went away for a while," Serafina said on her way to the cupboard for mugs.

"You could have told me that!" Dielle said, glaring at her. "I was worried about you! No one has seen you in ages!"

"I'm sorry! I just needed some time by myself. Tell me, how is your mother?"

Dielle collapsed onto a chair. "Not very good. I left

today while she was taking a nap, but I can't be gone for long."

"How are your reading and writing coming?"

"Pretty well, I think. I brought the book you gave me. There are some words I don't understand."

"Let me see," Serafina said as she poured tea into the mugs. She wished that she could offer Dielle cider, but she was short on supplies and didn't have anything else to drink.

Serafina helped her friend figure out some words but not as many as she'd expected. They were looking at the last few pages when Maks jumped onto the table, knocking over the cane that had been leaning against Serafina's chair.

Dielle reached to pick up the cane. "Where did you get this?" she asked Serafina. "I've never seen wood quite like it before."

"A giant gave it to me. He's a friend of mine. I met him on a cliff by the sea. I met a wood nymph there, too."

Dielle shook her head in amazement. "First fairies, now a giant and a wood nymph. You are so lucky!" When Maks bumped into Dielle's shoulder with his head, she handed the cane to Serafina and began to scratch the cat behind his ears. "And then there's this handsome fellow! I wish I had a cat just like him."

"Sorry," said Serafina. "I can't give him away. He goes with the cottage." When Maks gave her a reproachful look, she hurried to add, "And I wouldn't even if I could. I've grown very fond of him."

Maks closed his eyes halfway and flicked his tail so it was standing straight up, making Serafina think she had said exactly the right thing.

Soon after Dielle left, a man came to Serafina's door, ready to ask a question. A flurry of visitors over the next few days made Serafina age so much that she decided she couldn't afford to stay in one spot; she *had* to find the blue rose tea as quickly as possible! She began to move from place to place, never staying anywhere for more than a few days, asking the people who came to visit her if they had ever seen blue roses. No one was able to help her.

Every time the cottage moved, Serafina searched the woods, fields, and stream banks nearby, hoping to find a fairy, but she never caught even a glimpse of one. Although she aged with each question she answered and she had more aches and pains every day, Serafina didn't want to give up. A month later, she was still no closer to finding blue roses, blue rose tea, or a fairy to ask about Summer Rose.

As time went on, fewer people came to see her. Young

men were off at war, leaving behind women and daughters to care for the too young, too old, or too infirm. Fearful, many refused to come out of their homes, even to see Baba Yaga.

After a week of traveling from one war-ravaged village to another without meeting anyone, Serafina was more discouraged than ever. Although a few of the villages had been left untouched, most showed evidence that some fighting had taken place, leaving behind destroyed buildings and a feeling of desolation. One day when the cottage settled in a new location, Serafina opened the door to find that ash filled the air, turning everything gray and making it difficult to breathe. Closing the door behind her, she shuffled to the bed and sat down.

"Chicken hut, chicken hut, take me away," she told the cottage. "And be gentle when you go."

Maks yawned and stretched his paws in front of him. "Are you trying to go anywhere in particular?"

"No," said Serafina. "I'd tell the cottage to go somewhere that hasn't seen any fighting, but it doesn't seem to know the difference."

"We could go somewhere far from people. I'd really like a nice meal of vole."

"We can't go into hiding again! Don't you

understand? I have to find blue roses so I can get my life back!"

"No need to bite my head off as if I were a stupid mouse! It was just a suggestion."

"I know, and I'm sorry. I guess I just don't have much patience anymore. I don't know if it's because I'm getting older or because I'm frustrated."

"You *are* very wrinkly," said Maks. "I've seen cantaloupes with smoother skin than yours."

Serafina's hands flew to her cheeks. Feeling the soft wrinkles, she sighed and dropped her hands to her lap. "You're right, but it's been ages since I looked in the mirror."

Grasping the cane that Auster had made for her, Serafina leveraged herself to her feet and started for the cupboard. She used the corner of her shawl to wipe old fingerprints off the mirror as she carried it to the window. After turning into the light, she held up the mirror to study her reflection. She'd lost weight since the last time she looked, and her wrinkles were more deeply etched. Her hair was still thick, but it was pure white now. Her hands looked older, too; the skin on the back of her hands was looser and as thin as parchment.

The cottage lurched and Serafina staggered. Maybe

the cat was right about going somewhere far from people, even if for only a few days.

"Chicken hut, chicken hut, take me to a place far from any town or village," Serafina said in a loud voice, then braced herself against the cupboard when the cottage changed direction. "I'm going to take a nap now," she told the cat as she shuffled toward her bed. "You might as well sleep, too, so you'll be ready to hunt when we get there."

* * *

Serafina was making her breakfast the next morning when the cottage slowed and abruptly settled to the ground. She had thought she'd heard a commotion outside just before the cottage stopped, but it was quiet now and she wasn't sure that she had heard correctly.

"Where do you think we are?" she asked Maks as she hobbled toward the window. The glass was so ash-covered from the previous stop that she couldn't see out.

"I don't know," said the cat, jumping to the top of the trunk and batting at the glass with his paw. "I smell trees and grass and mice and . . ."

The bones were already pouring out the door when the cat added, ". . . men and horses and— Shut that door, Baba Yaga!"

She stopped, stunned, halfway to the door. The

cottage had brought them to a valley she had visited before. Normally it was a peaceful place where her only visitors were rabbits, deer, and occasionally a curious bear. Now, however, the lush grass was trampled from horses' hooves and ragged shoes. Men caught in the throes of battle had stopped in midswing at the arrival of the house on chicken legs. It was as if the world had frozen and was waiting to see what she would do.

Serafina shuffled to the threshold and peered out the door. She had never seen so many people looking at her at once, some in fear and some as if her arrival was wondrous. Then suddenly everyone began to move again. Many of the men returned to wielding their swords or maces or axes, galloping their horses from one fray to another, or turning where they stood to slash at their opponents. Others fled from the field, dodging the men who were still fighting. But there were those who turned to their officers as if to learn what to do. It seemed that in their minds, Baba Yaga's arrival had changed something.

Serafina watched, unable to move, as the officers rallied their men. She could see two distinct groups now. Those who followed the standard bearing the griffin-and-bear design of King Borysko wore splashes of crimson on their helms, while the men hurrying to the standard bearing a kraken wore a muddy green.

"King Kolenka's men," she said under her breath even as they raised the kraken high and charged in her direction.

"Shut the door!" screamed Maks.

Startled, Serafina dropped her cane. It fell to the floor with a clatter, landing across the threshold. She looked up as a wave of foot soldiers swept across the trampled grass, urged on by officers on horseback, the kraken standard waving above them. The field seethed as soldiers bearing the bear and griffin tried to stop King Kolenka's men, who were carrying the battle toward Serafina.

"Baba Yaga, get us out of here!" the cat yowled.

She was leaning down, reaching for her cane, when an arrow slammed into the doorframe, the breeze from its passing ruffling her hair. Grabbing the cane with fumbling fingers, she backed into the cottage and slammed the door behind her. "Chicken hut, chicken hut, take us far away!" she cried, stumbling toward the table.

Even as the cottage rose to its feet, arrows thrummed into the door. Serafina glanced toward the ceiling as more arrows struck the roof like lethal rain. Suddenly the door slammed open, admitting the bones and skulls. Arrows followed them into the room, but the bones turned, swatting them away from Serafina and out the still-open door. Instead of returning to the trunk, the skulls clustered around the doorway, screaming at the archers and gnashing their teeth until the door began to close.

When the door was finally shut, the skulls flew to the trunk, congratulating one another on their ferocity. Serafina was dismayed to see that arrows had cracked some of them and that Yure had an arrow protruding from his eye hole.

"You poor things!" she cried as the cottage strode away from the battlefield.

As the lid of the trunk closed, Maks glanced at it with disdain. "They're just numskulls. They can't feel a thing."

"But they tried to help me!" Serafina said. Shuffling to the cupboard, she took out her jar of skull polish, a clean rag, and a pot of glue. It was hard for her to sit on the floor, but she inched her way down, groaning. When she lifted the lid of the trunk, the skulls were all talking at once.

"Did you see how brave I was?" Krany asked the skull beside him. "I was just as brave when I was alive. Why, once in the heat of battle—"

"Is everyone all right?" Serafina asked the skulls.

"Right as rain," said a skull buried at the bottom of

the pile. "But could you please take out Yure's arrow? It's poking me something fierce."

"Of course," Serafina said, taking out the skull on top. "Why, you're all scratched! And you have an awful new crack!" she said to the skull below him. "It's going to take forever to polish you all again."

Serafina took out one skull at a time, checking their smooth surfaces for cracks. Some she rubbed with polish, erasing scratch marks as best she could. She used glue on cracked skulls and tried to find the missing pieces of those more badly damaged. As she returned each skull to its resting place, she thanked it for helping her.

"Aren't you going to thank me?" Maks asked as Serafina sank onto the bed, rubbing her aching back.

"You didn't do anything," she replied.

"Sure I did. I told you to shut the door."

"And that was supposed to be helpful? I'd already figured that out for myself."

"But you weren't doing it!" said the cat.

"And neither were you," Serafina said, turning her back on him.

* * *

They spent most of that day closed up in the cottage as it strutted across the kingdom. When they passed through a rainstorm, Serafina discovered that some of the arrows had made holes in the roof and it leaked in half a dozen places. She used the few pots and empty jugs she had to collect the dripping water.

It was early evening when the cottage stopped again. Although it had quit raining some time before, the pots and jugs were full and Serafina wanted to empty them. As soon as the floor of the cottage touched the ground, she opened the door, a sloshing pot in her hand. To her surprise, they had returned to Mala Kapusta.

Serafina was stunned. The town looked nothing like it had the last time she'd been there. Where well-kept shops and homes had lined the street, partial shells of buildings were all that remained. The sign that had hung over the tavern called the Bialy Jelen lay broken on the ground in front of the charred remains of the building. Parts of houses down the street were still intact, but none had been left completely unscathed.

The town seemed to be deserted, but Serafina had learned that often people remained behind in even the most ravaged areas, scratching a living out of the ruins as they waited to rebuild. Hungry and afraid, these people could be just as dangerous as enemy soldiers. Serafina decided that this would be another short visit; she would empty the pots and tell the cottage to leave.

She was pouring water out of a second pot when she glanced across the road. The tree that had held Alek's bouquets and letters was gone, probably chopped down when someone needed firewood. Numbed by all the destruction she had seen, she was still saddened at the thought that she would never again find letters from Alek in the hollow of that old apple tree. She was about to go back inside when she saw something fluttering on the ground near the tree's roots. Curious, she set the pot in front of her door and shuffled to the gate. "What are you doing?" Boris asked when she put her hand on the latch. "You shouldn't go out there!"

"I'm just going across the road," she told him.

"I don't think this is a good idea," the skull mumbled as she pushed the gate open.

Serafina sighed. "You can watch me the entire time. If you think something is wrong, holler and I'll come straight back."

She could hear the skull grumbling as she crossed the road, but she really didn't care. The sight of something that looked like a dried flower and a bit of faded ribbon made her hurry the last few feet. *Is it possible?* she thought, using the cane to push aside dry leaves. Serafina gasped when she saw what rested beneath. A withered bouquet lay on the ground where the tree had stood, and under it she spotted a rain-damaged letter.

Serafina's hands were shaking when she reached for the precious items. When she stood, her heart was pounding so fast that her body seemed to vibrate.

"Is that another letter?" called Boris. "Don't stand out there! Bring it back here to read."

Clutching the letter and bouquet to her chest, Serafina hobbled across the road and through the open gate. She walked only a few feet before stopping to examine the letter. The parchment was dry now, but at some time rain had soaked it, making the ink run and the writing on the outside almost illegible. Even so, she was convinced that the letters read *"Fina."*

She was unfolding the parchment when she heard a sound from the field across the street.

"Go inside!" shouted Boris, but then another voice rose above his.

"I know I can ask only one question of Baba Yaga, and I would ask that question now," called a voice Serafina knew better than any other.

She froze, her emotions so jumbled that she didn't know what to do. It was Alek, she was sure of it, and her heart sang with the knowledge that she was about to see him again. Only she didn't want *him* to see *her*, not like this. She held her breath as she slowly turned toward him, letting it out in a gasp when she saw his beloved face. He was battered and filthy, but he looked so wonderful that tears filled her eyes.

Although she was afraid that Alek would be horrified when he saw how she had aged, his expression never showed anything except how much he loved her. "Alek!" she cried. "I thought I might never see you again. How are you? Is my family all right? And your father—how is he?"

"Everyone is fine. It's you we're worried about. We want you home, Serafina, and I'll do whatever it takes to get you there. I've been trying to find someone who can tell me how to help you, and I finally realized that I already know that person. *You* can tell me if I ask the right question."

"Then ask me now," she said, trying to keep her voice steady.

Alek took a step closer, his gaze never leaving her face. "My question is—what must I do to turn you back into the girl I knew?"

Serafina shivered. Something had already changed. Someone had used his question to ask about her, knowing that he could ask only one question his entire life. "You have taken the first step by using your question for me," she replied. "The rest will not be so easy. Travel to the island called Paradise to ask the fairy Summer Rose for blue roses for my tea. Bring me a bushel of blue roses—enough to make tea for fifty years. Bring me the girl who will replace me as Baba Yaga—a girl who is the third daughter of a third daughter, who can read and write, and who is good of heart and sweet of soul. Bring me polish for my skulls and food for my cat, oil for my gate, and wood for my fire. Love me and believe in me, and you will have me back."

"Let me see if I have this right. I need to find blue roses, a girl, skull polish, cat food, oil, and firewood. I already love you and believe in you, so this shouldn't be too hard. Any idea where this island is located?"

Serafina shook her head. "I'm sorry. I'd never even heard of it until I said it just now."

"Don't worry. I'll find it. I probably just have to find the right map. Is there anything I can do for you in the meantime?"

"Hold me in your arms?" she said in an uncertain voice.

Alek had looked worried before, but now a smile lit up his eyes. "There's nothing I'd rather do." In four long strides, Alek was there with his strong arms wrapped around her as if holding her close would protect her from the world. "Where should I meet you when I have everything?" he asked.

"The cottage goes only to places it's visited many times before," Serafina told him. "This is the closest it will take me to Kamien Dom. I'll come back once a week and see if you are here."

"I'll return as soon as I can," Alek said. "And nothing will ever keep us apart again."

Serafina took a long, shuddering breath as a spark of hope began to grow inside her. Alek was there, he knew what he had to do now, and soon everything would be all right.

CHAPTER 16

Serafina had thought that saying good-bye to Alek was one of the hardest things she'd ever done, but she soon decided that waiting for his return was even harder. The cottage had taken her to the outskirts of one of the less damaged villages, where she planned to spend the week until she could go back to Mala Kapusta. Only a few days after her arrival, she learned that the war had ended. The decisive battle had taken place in Demetr's Valley, Demetr being the name of the first man to fall there. From the bits and pieces she heard from her visitors, Serafina was certain that it was the battle that she had witnessed. She wondered what had happened after she left.

Although she was still aging with each question she

answered, she felt calmer now, knowing in her heart that her time as Baba Yaga would soon be over. She wasn't the only one looking forward to what lay ahead. With the war over, she saw bedraggled groups of men on the roads, returning to their families. She saw women and children rushing to greet them and heard laughter for the first time in far too long. Men talked and joked as they tore down charred buildings and built new rawwood structures in their place. Women stood outside their homes, visiting with their neighbors while small children played at their feet. Serafina was surprised by how friendly people were and how many went out of their way to greet her.

One afternoon she was sweeping the cottage floor when Boris shouted that she had a visitor. Opening her door, she saw a woman standing by the gate, holding a small basket over her arm. Although the woman looked horrified when she had to lift the bone latch to come into the yard, she seemed to find the cottage fascinating, ogling it as she approached the door.

Handing Serafina the basket, she said, "Here you go. These fruit tarts are for you. I want the basket back."

"Won't you come in?" said Serafina, stepping out of the way so the woman could get past her.

"I'd love to," the woman said, her gaze darting from

the stove to the table to the bed. "It's a cozy cottage, perfect for a woman by herself. Wouldn't do for a family, though. Oh, look. You have a cat. No one mentioned that." With a rustle of full skirts, she swept toward the bed and reached out to pet Maks. The cat drew back and hissed, swiping at her with his claws. Jerking her hand away, the woman looked at Maks with distaste. "Not a very friendly animal. I wouldn't allow a cat like that in my house!"

Maks sat up on the bed and narrowed his eyes at her.

As Serafina hobbled to the table to set down the basket, the woman crossed to the cupboard and opened the door. "So many things for one person! This is different," she said, plucking a colorful jar from one of the top shelves.

"It's nothing special," Serafina said, moving as quickly as she could to the cupboard. Taking the jar from the woman, she returned it to the shelf, though it hurt her back to stretch so high. She had to nudge the woman out of the way to close the cupboard door. Stepping in front of it, she blocked the woman from opening it again. "So, did you come to ask me a question?"

"Oh no," said the woman. "I just came to meet you. I've heard about Baba Yaga from so many people that I thought it was time I saw you myself."

Serafina blinked, not sure what to make of that. The woman made her sound more like an oddity than a person.

"I never did believe in you," the woman said, turning to Serafina. "No one in their right mind did. I mean, the same people who believe in fairies or wood nymphs or those horrible Vilas who supposedly kill hunters believe in Baba Yaga, and we all know how naive and unsophisticated people like that are. But then when the prince made his announcement! Why, that changed everything! I mean, if the prince says Baba Yaga is real, then she must be. Er, I mean, you must be."

"What announcement?" asked Serafina.

"So, as I understand it, if I ask you a question, you'll tell me the truth, which could be horrible or wonderful, depending on the question. And I get to ask only one question my entire life, so it should be something very important."

Serafina nodded. "That's true."

"Well, I don't know what my important question will be yet, so if I say something that sounds like a question, don't pay it any mind."

"I can't do that," Serafina told her. "If you ask me a question, I *will* answer it and it *will* be your only one."

"Then I'd better be careful what I say!" the woman

said with a laugh. "You should offer me tea. People who visited you told me that you do that sometimes."

"Well, yes, but . . ."

The woman crossed to the table and pulled out the seat where Baba Yaga always sat. "Take your time," she said, sitting down. "We have so many things to talk about."

"We do?" Serafina said as she opened the cupboard door to take out two cups. She glanced back when she heard a retching sound. Maks was sitting beside the woman's foot, coughing up a hairball onto her shoe.

The woman shifted in the seat, moving her feet out of the way. She gave the cat a disgusted look and turned back to Serafina. "Everyone says that you consulted with Prince Cynrik and predicted that he would win the war."

Serafina shut the cupboard door to face her guest. "That's not exactly—"

"My husband was at Demetr's Valley. The night before the battle, Prince Cynrik told everyone about it."

"Oh, really?"

The woman nodded. Her gaze fell on Serafina's book, and she reached for it across the table. Serafina moved faster than she had in ages, slamming the two cups down on the table and grabbing the book from the woman's hands.

"Well!" said the woman, an injured expression on her face.

The cat jumped up on the table and glared at the woman while Serafina wrapped her arms around the book and shuffled to the other chair. Her back was really hurting now, and she'd pulled something in her leg when she'd moved so fast. "You were saying . . ."

"Oh, just that your little prediction boosted our men's spirits so much that they fought harder than ever. And then you turned up on the battlefield at precisely the right moment, and, well, our army couldn't help but win."

"I don't think that's—"

"Hmm," murmured the woman as she reached for the basket she'd brought. "If you're not going to eat these, I might as well." Opening the basket, she took out the larger of the two tarts and bit into it. A look of pleasure appeared on her face. "These are so good!" she said through a mouthful of food. "I'm an excellent cook. Anyway, everyone is saying that we won the war because of you, so it must be true."

Maks had started walking back and forth only inches from what was left of the woman's fruit tart, shedding a trail of black fur.

"I really don't think that—" Serafina began.

"What is wrong with that cat?" said the woman,

glaring at him. "Wait! That's not a question!" The dismayed expression on her face when she turned to Serafina was almost comical.

The cat sat down, looking satisfied when Serafina said in her Baba Yaga voice, "Nothing is wrong with the cat. He doesn't like you and thinks that you are a very rude person. He wants you to leave and is trying to make you go."

"Well, I never!" the woman said, getting to her feet. "And after I brought you such a delicious treat!" She was storming out the door, her basket in her hand, when she stopped suddenly and glanced back at Serafina. "Does this mean that you won't answer my question when I think of something important?"

"I'm afraid so," Serafina replied, not even trying to look sorry. After closing the door behind the woman, she shuffled to her chair and sat down with a groan. "So, according to her, more people believe in Baba Yaga now. I wonder if the prince's announcement will make it easier for my parents to believe in magic. Ah, I have to thank you," she told Maks, who had come over to rub against her. "I don't know how I would have gotten rid of her if you hadn't been here to help. You surprised me, though. I didn't know you could shed when you wanted to."

"There are a lot of things that you don't know about

me," said the cat. "For instance, did you know that I was able to get the last tart out of the basket before she left? If you don't want it, I'd be happy to eat it for you!"

* * *

Even though Serafina doubted that a week was long enough for Alek to find everything she needed, she couldn't keep from hoping that he'd be in Mala Kapusta when she arrived. When he wasn't, she went away for another week. The next time she returned, he still wasn't there. Although people had started rebuilding the town, Serafina spotted a group of rough-looking men and decided that she didn't feel safe. She left the town again. When she returned the third time, men were working on a new tavern, which was going to be larger than before.

Serafina stepped into her yard to look around, but there was still no sign of Alek. She stood watching the activity at the tavern for a few minutes before glancing across the road. The tree was gone, but Serafina was sure she spotted blue ribbon draped across the stump. Alek must have left her a message!

Serafina moved at a much slower pace now, her aging bones and muscles unable to carry her as quickly as her still-young mind wanted to go. As she hobbled across the road, leaning on her cane, she thought about the first time she'd found a letter from Alek in the tree. "The world was so different then," she murmured. When she saw a blue ribbon tied around a piece of parchment, her heart jumped and she felt almost young again.

Serafina was bending down, reaching for the parchment, when she heard a sound. Thinking it might be Alek, she turned around, a smile on her face.

It wasn't Alek. Three rough-looking men had emerged from the tavern, and all of them were staring at her as they walked in her direction. When they saw her looking their way, they stopped trying to be quiet and began to run across the street.

"Come back inside the fence quickly!" shouted Boris.

But Serafina's body was too weak to be quick. She had taken only a few steps when the men were upon her, hustling her into a carriage that had emerged from behind the tavern. The skulls began to scream the instant the men touched her, making town dogs howl and a flock of crows take to the air. A burly man with shaggy brown hair and a thick red beard followed her through the carriage door and sat on the seat across from her, closing the door behind him and muting the racket of the skulls, who hadn't stopped screaming. With the coachman's shout and crack of a whip, the horses started off.

"What do you want of me?" Serafina asked the man.

"Nothing," he replied. "It's Lord Zivon who wants you. I'm just taking you to him."

"I've never met Lord Zivon. Why would he do this?"

The man snorted and shook his head. "You insulted the man and made him angrier than I've ever seen him, but you don't even know who he is. You met him once months ago."

"My memory isn't as good as it used to be," she said, although it wasn't true. "Please, if you would be so kind, at least tell me what he looks like?"

"You'll know soon enough," said the man, ignoring her when she tried to talk to him again.

Chapter 17

Since the man refused to talk to Serafina for the rest of the trip, she was left to figure out which of her visitors was Zivon. She knew that she had angered some people with her answers, but only a few had acted as if they hated her enough to have her kidnapped. And there was that man who had sent those awful people to grab her in the marketplace. Could Zivon have been trying to abduct her even then?

It was dark when the carriage finally rolled to a stop and the man opened the door to jump down. Although the sign was gone from the front of the building, Serafina thought that it had probably once been an inn. She was still eyeing the building and the people lounging outside when the man who had ridden with her reached into the carriage and picked her up as if she were no heavier than a sack of potatoes. Crinkling her nose at his sour smell, she struggled to get down and even tried thumping him with her cane. The man cursed under his breath and took the cane from her. After tossing it to the ground, he carried her out of the carriage to the door of the inn.

"Here she is, Chorly," he said, setting her down just inside the door.

Serafina glanced at this second man. He had a long burn mark on his face and he was scowling as if he had seen something loathsome. "That's her, all right," said Chorly. "She's older now, but I'd remember her anywhere. Take her downstairs."

Hefting her over his shoulder again, the man who had abducted Serafina carried her down a set of rickety stairs to a cool, dark room where a smoking torch mounted on the wall provided the only light. After setting her on a wooden bench, he plodded up the stairs, closing the door at the top behind him.

Rubbing her ribs where they'd pressed into the man's shoulder, Serafina studied the room. She could tell that she was in a root cellar from the barrels lined up against one wall and the few dried apples and pieces of broken carrot on the dirt floor. The room was chilly and smelled like soil and onions and had the musty odor peculiar to old storage spaces. She shivered and wrapped her arms around herself, hoping that her captors wouldn't make her stay down there for long.

The door above opened, and Serafina looked up to see feet descending one slow step at a time. As the man came farther down the stairs, she saw that it was Chorly with a candle in his hand. He was limping badly, and suddenly Serafina remembered him screaming as he fell out of her lurching cottage. This man had been one of the thieves who had forced their way into her home.

Chorly had almost reached the bottom of the stairs when three others clattered down behind him. Serafina watched as a taller man came forward and the light of the candle fell on his face. The scar crossing his lips looked even more sinister in the flickering light than it had inside her cottage.

"I wondered when I'd see you again," he said. "I'm glad I didn't kill you the last time we met. You're going to be quite useful."

"How is that?" asked Serafina. "Do you want me to answer a question for Lord Zivon?"

One side of the man's lips pulled back in a scornful sneer. "You already answered a question for me, remember? It wasn't even the one I really wanted."

"You're Zivon?" she said, sounding surprised. "I thought you were a thief."

"*Lord* Zivon," he corrected her, his eyes turning cold and hard. "We all play different roles when necessary. And now your role requires that you answer questions. Chorly, who is our first volunteer?"

Handing the candle to one of the other men, Chorly limped to the bottom of the stairs and barked an order at someone standing above. A thin man with a dirty bandage wrapped around his head crept down the stairs. He kept his eyes on Lord Zivon like a mouse might watch a cat. When the man paused at the bottom of the steps, Chorly shoved him toward Serafina, saying, "Go ahead. Ask your question."

The man stumbled into her, then took two steps back and turned so he could still see Lord Zivon. Wetting his lips with his tongue, he said in a shaky voice, "Did you really tell Prince Cynrik that he would win?"

"I told him what he would need to do to end the war," Serafina said in her Baba Yaga voice.

Lord Zivon nodded. "Pay him off, Chorly."

Chorly handed a coin to the one who had asked the question and then motioned toward the door. The paid man scurried up the stairs without a backward glance. A moment later another man came down the stairs to take his place. Dressed in homespun clothes and dirty sandals, he looked like a farmer.

"Go ahead," said Chorly.

The man hesitated, looking down at Serafina, who could see the indecision in his eyes. Before he could begin, she met his gaze directly and said, "You do know that if you ask me a question on Lord Zivon's behalf, you'll never be able to ask me one of your own? Is it really worth a coin to lose the chance to ask me something that is important to you?"

"Don't listen to her," snapped Lord Zivon. "Ask the question before I lose my patience."

The man bit his lip. Taking a deep breath, he said all in a rush, "King Borysko has signed a treaty with King Kolenka, but he's labeled Lord Zivon as a traitor. He has already confiscated Lord Zivon's lands and robbed him of his titles. What must Lord Zivon do to get his lands and titles back?"

"Because of Lord Zivon's heinous crimes, there is nothing he can do to regain his lands, his titles, or his position in King Borysko's eyes," Serafina said in her Baba Yaga voice. "However, in three generations' time, a member of Zivon's line will distinguish himself in battle fighting for King Borysko's descendant. Some of Zivon's lands will be returned to his descendant then."

No one looked happy about her answer, least of all Zivon. As Chorly hustled the farmer from the room, Zivon's sneer became more pronounced. "That answer must make you very happy."

"Not at all," said Serafina. "I just give the answers. They have nothing to do with me."

"I'm sure you were happy to tell Cynrik how to win."

Serafina shook her head. "I don't like it when people fight for any reason."

The sound of thudding feet came from above. Chorly whispered into Lord Zivon's ear, and then all the men climbed the stairs, taking the candle with them. One of them shut the door, and Serafina was left alone, straining to hear any sound. She doubted that Zivon was finished with her yet.

Minutes passed as she listened to people moving above her. Then suddenly it was quiet and she wondered if they had gone. Serafina eyed the stairs, thinking about how hard it would be to climb them, but before she'd gotten up from the bench, the door creaked open and closed again.

Serafina held her breath as the burly man who had carried her into the room came down the stairs. "I've come to ask you a question," he said in a near whisper, "but we have to be quick. There's no telling when they'll be back. My friends and I want to know—what will happen to us if we stay with Lord Zivon?"

Serafina sighed. She was getting frailer with each question, and her back now had a pronounced curve. Speaking in her Baba Yaga voice, she said, "If you stay with Zivon, you and your friends will be hunted down like wild beasts and die in disgrace. Should you leave now, you can return to your families and no one will know that you sided with a traitor."

The man nodded as if she had confirmed something he was already thinking. "Then we'd best go now before Zivon comes back," he said. "He isn't going to like this one bit."

He was halfway up the stairs again when Serafina called out, "If you're leaving, could you take me with you?"

The man stopped long enough to shake his head. "If I leave, he'll be angry, but he won't come after me. If I take you with me, he'd hunt us both down, but I'm the one he'd kill."

This time when he shut the door, Serafina could hear the scrape of a bolt as he locked the door behind him. She rubbed her arms again, trying to chafe away the chill. With the door locked, there wasn't much use climbing the stairs. She'd just have to wait for another opportunity.

Serafina must have dozed off, because the next thing she knew, men were shouting upstairs and making the floor above her shake as they ran. She wondered how long it would be before they came to see her again and wasn't surprised when Zivon came running down the steps, stopping partway when he saw that she was still there.

"Did my men talk to you while I was gone?" he demanded, scowling.

"Yes," she said.

"And what did you tell them?"

"Very little."

Zivon came down the rest of the steps, glaring at her the whole way. "If you don't answer my questions, old woman, I'll have Chorly make you, and there's nothing he'd like better."

There really wasn't any point in keeping it a secret. Zivon had probably already guessed what had happened and just wanted her to confirm it. "I told them the truth, of course. Then the man said that he and his friends were going to leave."

Zivon swore under his breath, glaring at Serafina as

if he wanted to throttle her. "You are not to talk to my men anymore."

"I can't help but answer their first questions," she warned.

"They won't be asking you anything," he declared, and turned to go back up the stairs.

Although Zivon closed the door behind him, Serafina could make out some of what he shouted at his men. No one was to speak to her at all, and anyone who dared to ask her a question would have to deal with him.

Once again she was left alone, and once again she dozed. The torch was guttering and about to go out when Chorly brought down a chunk of stale bread and a bowl of cold boiled cabbage. He also brought her a thin blanket, which she wrapped around herself, grateful for even that small bit of warmth. Chorly looked at her as if daring her to try to talk to him, but all she did was thank him and start nibbling the bread.

Sitting alone in the quiet cellar, Serafina found her mind wandering. She remembered Widow Zloto's warnings about bad luck and how everyone had laughed at her superstitions. Maybe the old woman had been right. Maybe her superstitions really did tell people how to avoid bad luck. Viktor's whistling in the tavern could have been the start, but whatever the cause, Serafina's luck couldn't have gotten much worse. If only Widow Zloto had spent as much time talking about good luck as she had about bad, Serafina might have figured out a way to change her luck.

Something scurried in the dark corner of the cellar, and Serafina turned to look behind her. *Rats*, she thought. *This cellar is probably full of them.* Pulling the blanket tighter around her shoulders, she lay down on the bench, not wanting to sleep on the floor if there were rats.

Serafina dreaded the long, cold night ahead. She had so much on her mind that she was certain she wasn't going to be able to sleep. Since the day Alek asked his question, she'd been excited about the future, but now she had nothing ahead of her except whatever terrible thing Zivon had planned. Even if she didn't die of old age soon, she doubted he was going to let her go. And because no one knew where she was, no one was going to come looking for her.

Chapter 18

Serafina dozed off and on that night and finally woke to the sound of hesitant footsteps on the stairs. Rubbing her eyelids, she turned her head to look up. A pool of torchlight spilled down the steps, growing larger as the person carrying it came nearer. It was Chorly with another man close behind him.

Serafina shivered. Stiff and sore, she sat up slowly as Chorly replaced the torch on the wall with a fresh one.

"Payment first," he told the man who had followed him down. Holding out his hand, Chorly gave the other man an expectant look.

The new man handed him some coins, then waited until he and Serafina were alone before saying, "If it's true that you're Baba Yaga, I have a question for you."

"Go ahead," she said, suddenly certain of the fate Zivon had planned for her. If he had his way, she would stay locked in his cellar for the rest of her life so that people had to pay him before they could ask her their question.

"My father buried his gold on his farm before the war. He died just before the war ended without telling us where to find the gold."

"And your question?" said Serafina.

"Where's the gold?" said the man, sounding impatient.

The man's question reminded Serafina so much of similar questions she'd been asked in the past that she felt as if in some ways nothing had changed. After answering him in her Baba Yaga voice, she thought about asking him for help, but from the occasional creak at the top of the stairs, she was fairly sure that Chorly was listening. Her captors had also learned where the gold was buried.

Three more people with questions came down the stairs in quick succession after that. All three wanted to know about lost relatives. After the third one left, Chorly brought Serafina more stale bread and a mug of tepid water. She spent the rest of the day seeing one person after another. By the time the last person left, she was so tired she could scarcely keep her eyelids from drifting shut. Her joints ached and her knuckles were swollen. Glancing at her hands, she saw that her fingers were no longer straight. Answering so many questions was making her body age faster than it ever had before.

When the door at the top of the stairs opened again, the smell of roasting meat wafted into the cellar. Serafina perked up, looking forward to dinner. Time seemed to crawl as she waited for Chorly, but when he came down the stairs, all he brought was cold boiled cabbage. She knew it would do no good to protest.

* * *

The next two days were just like the first. So many people came to see Serafina that she began to wonder how the men were finding them all. Some paid with coins; others brought old family jewelry, treasured bits of lace, even a pair of good shoes.

Although more than one person asked her how to find a family fortune, the most-asked questions were about missing relatives and friends. Each piece of bad news she gave depressed her even as it made her body age; she dreaded seeing the next person on the stairs. Her hearing was getting bad, and she had to ask people to repeat their questions. Tiring easily, she dozed between visitors, waking when Chorly shook her shoulder. Her back hurt so much that it was hard to get comfortable, and her knees were sore all the time. She was so achy that walking was a chore, although she tried to pace when she was alone at night before the torch went out, hoping to relieve some of the stiffness in her legs. If she was going to escape, she would have to do it soon.

By the afternoon of the fourth day, the number of people coming to see Serafina had trickled to a few each hour. Chorly didn't seem happy at the decline in income, and she wondered just how long she would be allowed to live once there was no one left to ask questions. Although Chorly still hadn't had a conversation with her since Zivon ordered him not to, at least he hadn't been uncivil. Now he was becoming abrupt with her, showing little patience when she dozed off or needed a question repeated.

"You can't blame me!" she finally said when he snapped at her. "My body gets older every time I answer a question."

"I can blame you for whatever I want," Chorly snarled. "It's your fault I have a gimpy leg. Your cottage dumped me out and I broke my leg in three places!"

Serafina closed her mouth and turned away.

* * *

Late that afternoon, Serafina was answering another farmer's question when they heard a commotion upstairs. Men shouted and ran across the floor overhead, shaking the floorboards so that dirt filtered down from the ceiling of the root cellar. She was still talking when Chorly bellowed from the top of the stairs, "Dorek, forget the crazy old bat and come up here now!"

Serafina's visitor looked nervous, but he waited for her to finish, his gaze flitting from her to the stairs and back again. When she stopped talking, he pelted up the steps as fast as he could move. Listening intently, she did not think she heard the door close behind him.

It was quiet now, without even the usual creak of people walking from room to room overhead.

Serafina struggled to her feet. She was weak, as much from poor food as from the magical aging, and the walk to the stairs was long and slow. Her feet were unsteady and her balance was poor; if only she still had her cane! When she finally reached the steps, she looked to the top and saw light through the open doorway. The inn itself was quiet, although she could hear that something was going on outside.

Gripping the railing with both hands, she raised her right foot up a step, then her left to the same step. Ever so slowly, she climbed the stairs, afraid that at any moment someone would appear in the doorway. She paused often to rest, but no one came and she finally reached the top unnoticed.

The noises outside had grown louder as she climbed the stairs, and now she could hear them quite clearly. It was the sound of battle—men shouting, horses screaming, the clash of swords, and the pounding of hooves. Standing at the top of the stairs, Serafina peered into the doorways of the rooms around her. The dining hall, the kitchen, and a storage room stood silent and empty.

She saw her cane leaning against a nearby wall. Weary from her climb, she shuffled across the floor to wrap her fingers around the stout wooden stick. The cane made walking easier as she crept to the front door and looked out.

It had been dark when she'd arrived at the inn, and she hadn't been able to see much. Now she could see that it was a stopover on a lonely stretch of road far from any towns. The forest had been cut back to accommodate the inn, a stable, and a small fenced field. A cow and two horses stood in the field, watching the men who had broken part of the fence as their fight moved down the road.

Serafina was considering hiding in the woods until the fighting was over when she noticed that one of the knights had raised his helm to wipe the sweat from his face. It was Prince Cynrik, looking older and more worn than the fresh-faced young man who had come to see her.

The prince had lowered his helm and ridden back into the fray when a horse at the edge of the fighting reared, dumping its rider on the ground. Serafina gasped when she saw that the man who had fallen off his horse was her father. Master Divis was trying to catch his mount's reins when the fighting surged in his direction. A big man, taller and broader than the rest, hurried to stand between Serafina's father and Zivon's men. She recognized Alek, who was wearing a boiled leather vest and wielding the biggest broadsword she'd ever seen. Toman Damek, the man who used to be the sheriff from Vioska, was there as well, running to help defend Serafina's father.

Serafina watched as Alek drove three of Zivon's men back, raining blows on them with his broadsword. The fighting had moved far enough into the field to trap two loose horses in a corner. Frightened, one of the horses knocked a man down and galloped across the field, throwing up clods of dirt with his hooves as he came between Alek and the men he was fighting. When two of the men backed away from the horse, they met Toman

Damek, who came after them with his sword. Serafina watched until Alek fought the last man so fiercely that the man turned and ran away.

Relieved that Alek was able to defend himself so well, Serafina headed around the side of the inn. Although she couldn't do anything directly for Alek or the others herself, she had an idea that just might help.

Serafina was staggering when she reached the back of the inn. Chickens scratched the ground outside a coop only a few yards away. Beyond that, the clearing extended another hundred feet to the forest that loomed dark and unwelcoming.

Locked in the root cellar, Serafina had been certain that she was going to die soon. Even so, she had tried to remember what she had learned about her abilities as Baba Yaga, hoping that one of them might help her. There was something that the cat had said that she hadn't thought much of at the time, but now it made her wonder. Maks had told her that the cottage and Baba Yaga were linked and that she could tell it what to do. She had thought that meant she could tell it when to go or how to walk. Now she wondered if it might mean more than that and just how strong that link might be.

Serafina reached the edge of the woods, prepared to hide if Zivon or one of his men came looking for her.

Turning around so that she faced the clearing, she declared in a loud voice, "Chicken hut, chicken hut, come here to me as quickly as you can!"

"And now," she said, stepping deeper into the shadows, "all I can do is wait."

CHAPTER 19

Serafina sat on the ground with her back against the broad trunk of an old maple. She could barely hear the fighting, the sound muted by the trees and her failing hearing. Exhausted and aching all over, she dozed after a time, her eyes shifting behind their lids as she dreamed of happier days. She saw Alek's laughing face as they ran hand in hand to their favorite pond one summer afternoon. She saw her sisters arguing good-naturedly as they shelled peas for supper. She saw her parents seated in front of the fireplace, sharing stories about what had happened that day. She saw the cat curled up on the bed in a patch of sunlight as the cottage strode from one place to another. And she saw the giant's smile when he learned that he might be able to see his family again.

"I found her," said the giant, which didn't quite fit in with her dream.

Serafina stirred when strong arms picked her up as gently as if she were an infant, but she didn't open her eyes. She turned her head toward the coarse fabric of a tunic when the same arms carried her through a doorway, but she still didn't open her eyes. Even when the arms lay her down on a familiar bed, she kept her eyes closed. It wasn't until Maks jumped up beside her and she felt his rough tongue on her cheek that she blinked her eyes open.

"You're here!" she cried as she struggled to sit up. When she glanced out the window and saw that the sun was still shining, she turned back to Maks. "I didn't expect you so soon. And you brought Auster!"

The giant was crouched in the corner, bent nearly double under the too-low ceiling. When Serafina looked his way, he grinned and waved, knocking the broom propped against the wall halfway across the room. "Oops!" he said, looking sheepish. "Sorry!"

"That's all right," said Serafina. "I'm just surprised that you fit through the doorway."

Auster rubbed the top of his head and his smile grew broader. "It wasn't easy."

"What did you do after those men kidnapped me?" Serafina asked Maks. "How did you end up with Auster?"

The cat licked his paw, then inspected it closely. "You aren't the only one with a link to the cottage," he said, sounding smug. "When the Baba Yaga is gone or unable to take control, I can tell the cottage what to do. After the men carried you off, some of their cronies tried to break into the cottage, so I told it to go somewhere safe. It went to the cliff where you met Auster. When a nymph came looking for you, I said you weren't there and told her what had happened. She left and sent your giant friend to me. We were talking about what we should do next when I decided to see if the special link the cottage has with you would help. I told the cottage to go find you, but I don't think it would have worked if you hadn't done something Baba Yaga–ish."

Serafina nodded. "I did answer a lot of questions over the last few days, although fewer people came today."

"That explains it. The cottage walked to this forest and kept circling. Then all of a sudden it started running."

"That was probably when I called to it," said Serafina.

242

The distant sound of shouting finally caught her attention, and everything came back to her at once. She wasn't dreaming and the men were still fighting! Serafina stood up so abruptly that she knocked Maks over. "You can tell me later! We have to go help Alek, and my father, and the prince, and Toman Damek!"

"What do they have to do with anything?" asked Maks.

"They're fighting the men who kidnapped me, the same ones who broke into the cottage. Zivon was behind it all! Chicken hut, chicken hut, get on your feet and hurry!"

Serafina grabbed hold of the headboard as the cottage scrambled to its feet. She waited until the floor had leveled off before she shuffled across the room to look out the window. "Go toward the road and look for the inn. That's it over there!" she shouted. "Go left to where those men are hacking at one another with swords. Very good! Now stomp around. I want you to scare them but not actually hurt anyone."

"Which one is Alek?" Auster asked, peering out the window beside her. Although he was kneeling on the floor, he was still taller than Serafina.

"There, the handsome one fighting the man with the red cap. Oh no! Alek, look out!"

Although most of the men on the field were running from the cottage stomping around on chicken legs, the man fighting Alek wasn't one of them. He was swinging his sword with all his might when Alek jumped out of the way.

Auster grunted and walked to the door, still bent over. "I can put an end to this," he said, and tried to lift the latch. When it wouldn't open, he gave it a shake and bellowed, "Open your door, hut, or I'll rip it off!"

The door opened with a crash, hitting the storage trunk behind it and bouncing back. Auster put up one hand and blocked the door from closing again. The hut was still stomping across the battlefield when the giant shuffled to the threshold and jumped, landing upright with a ground-shaking *whump!* that made everyone stop and stare.

"Enough!" he bellowed loud enough to make the cottage walls rattle. "The next man to swing a sword is going to answer to me! Drop your weapons now!"

There was a loud clatter as every man on the field dropped his weapon. Serafina noticed that even her father, who wasn't carrying a weapon, stared down at his hands as if he wished he had something to drop.

"Where's the prince?" Auster demanded as the men in front backed away from him.

Prince Cynrik nudged his horse toward the giant with Toman Damek close behind. "I'm right here!" called the prince.

"If Zivon knows what's good for him, he'll admit defeat and his men will turn themselves in. When they do, your people can round them up."

"It would help if my men had their weapons back," the prince said with a twist to his lips.

"Fine," said the giant. "But no more fighting!"

Serafina told the hut to settle to the ground as the prince and his men rounded up Zivon's followers. Once the bones had hurtled from the cottage and made their fence, Maks sauntered outside to watch what was going on. Serafina was about to go as well, but when she patted her hair, she found it was a tangled mess. It was bad enough that Alek was going to see her looking so old; she didn't want to look disheveled, too. After brushing her hair and tidying her rumpled clothes, she took the time to look in her mirror. The face that looked back was the oldest she had ever seen. Even her grandmother had looked younger than this before she died.

"It can't be helped," Serafina said, touching one white

eyebrow and running her fingers down the soft wrinkles of her cheek.

She was walking out the door when Boris shouted, "Baba Yaga, you have company!"

"I can see that," Serafina said, smiling shyly at her visitor.

Alek was standing just outside her gate like all the visitors who had come with a question. "I have everything you asked for, Fina," he said, and turned to gesture behind him. A farmer's wagon rumbled out of the trees where it had been hidden during the fighting. The back of the wagon was filled with barrels.

Jumping onto the bed of the wagon, Alek took the dagger from his belt and pried off a barrel's lid. Serafina was holding her breath when he reached in and took out a single, perfect blue rose. "You said that finding the island called Paradise wouldn't be easy and you were right! I climbed a mountain to ask a wise man where to find the island. Then I had to cross three rivers, slog through a swamp, and steal a boat from an ogre. Once I reached the island, I found Summer Rose. She said you told her about me, so she was glad to help. She gave me a magic potion to use on bushes that produce white roses. One drop of potion and all its roses turn blue. When I got back I heard how you had helped

246

Prince Cynrik, so I went to his castle. He let me change nearly every white rosebush in his kingdom. Now Baba Yaga will never run out of blue roses again!"

"Alek, I can't believe you did it!" cried Serafina.

"And that's not all," said Alek. "When you said that you needed one barrel, I was afraid that might not be enough to make tea for fifty years, so I filled ten." Dipping his hand into the open barrel, he scooped out a handful of roses to show her. "I also brought polish for skulls, food for a cat, oil for a gate, and wood for a fire." Alek gestured to some of the other barrels, then turned to a hooded figure seated beside the driver. "And here is the next Baba Yaga."

The figure pushed back her hood, revealing Dielle's smiling face.

"Dielle?" said Serafina. "Are you sure you want to do this?"

Dielle nodded and her smile grew broader. "I am the third daughter of a third daughter. My mother had two baby girls before she had me, but neither of them lived more than a few days. I've gotten good at reading and writing, which you said might be one of the reasons your aunt chose you to be the next Baba Yaga."

"I remember," said Serafina.

"Mother died right before the war ended. Once she

was gone, I no longer had to stay in our cottage. When I heard that someone was looking for blue roses, I knew that he was trying to help you. I went after Alek and caught up with him when he was on his way to the mountain to talk to the wise man. I told him that we were friends and that I admired you so much and wished I could do what you did someday. He sent me to your parents' house to wait for his return. When Alek got word to us that he had gone to the prince's castle, your father and I went to join him. I really want to be the next Baba Yaga. My mother is dead and Danya never came back from the war. I can go anywhere I want to now, but what I want more than anything is to help people the way you helped me and Mother. Besides, you know how much I love Maks," she said, smiling at the cat, who had come to see what was going on.

"Sometimes the things you tell people aren't what they want to hear," said Serafina.

"I know. I've heard about some of the things you've told them. Even so, I know I would make a very good Baba Yaga."

"If you're sure . . . ," said Serafina. "But first I have to see if this tea works. No one can be Baba Yaga for long if it doesn't."

Dielle hopped down from the wagon and followed

Serafina inside to watch while she put water on to boil. Maks sauntered in behind them and jumped onto the bed. Dielle plopped down beside the cat. "I have something for you," she told him, opening a pouch she had hanging from her belt. Maks stretched his neck to sniff her hand.

"You do like fish, don't you?" she asked, holding her hand closer.

Serafina could hear Maks purring from the other side of the room as he nibbled the fish from Dielle's hand and licked her fingers thoroughly.

"I thought you'd like that," Dielle told the cat, scratching him behind his ears. "I made sure we brought a whole barrel of dried fish as part of the cat food."

The cat purred louder and got up to bump Dielle's pouch with his head. She giggled and reached for another piece of fish.

Serafina had just taken a cup out of the cupboard when her father stepped into the cottage. "Alek will be joining us soon," he said. "He's telling the men unloading the wagon what to do."

Setting the cup on the table, she turned to hug her father. He was thinner than he had been, and his brown hair was going gray, but he still smelled like she remembered and the whiskers on his cheeks still felt the same.

"My sweet girl!" he said, patting her back. He drew away to look at her, and his brow tightened in a scowl. "I heard that you looked older but not as old as this! You look older than I do now!"

"I lost the last of the tea and the fairy had gone away. My body kept aging and . . . Did Alek explain to you what it means to be Baba Yaga?"

"Yes, he did. He also told us what a Baba Yaga does. We had a hard time believing him at first, but when we heard what Prince Cynrik said before the big battle, we knew that Alek's story had to be true. Who would have thought that my little girl would be caught up in something like this!"

Serafina gave him another hug. "I've missed you so much, Father. I didn't think I'd ever see you again."

"I was never going to stop trying to get my baby girl back, Kitten," he said, kissing her cheek. "When I learned that Viktor let you go into a strange house alone and then left town without even trying to find out who had taken you, I could have throttled him!"

"Where is Viktor now?" Serafina asked, glancing toward the door.

"I have no idea," said her father. "He hired a serving girl to help your sister and ran off with the girl two months later. Your sister and her babies live with your mother and me, and we're happy to have them. Yevhen wanted to come with us, but I asked him to stay to keep watch over everyone at home. Have you spoken to Alek? He put everything he had into finding you. We would never have gotten this far if it hadn't been for him."

"I'll go see him, Father. Just as soon as I've had some tea."

Serafina was torn. She wanted to fling herself into Alek's arms more than anything, tell him how much she had missed him and how happy she was to see him, and thank him for everything he had done. But she wanted to drink the tea first so that she really was the Serafina he used to know and not the old woman with bones so frail that a strong hug might crack them. And what if the tea didn't work? Then no matter how much they wanted to be with each other, it wasn't going to happen. If that was the case, she wanted to know it now.

While Serafina dropped a rose into the cup and added the boiling water, her father took a seat at the table, where he nervously awaited the outcome of the tea. Not wanting to talk about what might or might not happen, Serafina stepped to the window to look outside but found herself watching Dielle instead. The girl was seated on the bed with Maks on her lap, studying the cottage, her eyes bright with curiosity.

Serafina's lips curved into a grim smile. Dielle would make an excellent Baba Yaga, but only if the tea worked. If the tea didn't make Serafina younger, she didn't want Dielle or any other girl to go through what she had and die an old lady when she should still have her whole life to live. At that moment, Serafina decided that if the tea didn't work, she would ask the fairy Summer Rose to help her find a way to be the last Baba Yaga.

"Do you think it's ready yet?" her father asked, leaning forward to peer into the cup.

Serafina nodded. "That should be good enough." Crossing to the table, she reached for the cup, her hand shaking. She had let the rose steep in the water for longer than she did with other types of tea, partly because she wanted to make sure the tea was strong enough and partly because she was afraid to try it. If it didn't work, Alek had gone to all that effort for nothing. If it didn't work, she would say good-bye to the people she loved and have the cottage take her far away for the little time she had left. If it didn't work . . .

She felt the change begin after the second sip. The aches and pains that had been her constant companions for weeks melted away like butter in a hot pan. The curve in her back straightened, and her limbs grew strong and steady. Her scalp tingled as her hair grew thicker and the color returned. Suddenly she could see and hear better. She glanced down at her hands as the soft wrinkles and brown spots disappeared and the skin became taut. Her clothes fit differently; things that had been loose were now tight. She blushed when she glanced down and saw the changes and realized that her father and Dielle were watching her.

"Fina?" said Alek. "Are you all right?" He had come into the cottage while she wasn't looking and was holding out his hand as if he wanted to touch her but was afraid.

"Oh yes," she told him, taking his hand in hers. "I'm better than all right! I feel wonderful! And it's all because of you, Alek!"

And suddenly she was in his arms and he was murmuring into her ear how much he loved her and had missed her and how he would have done anything to have her back. Serafina never wanted to let him go, but she also felt like dancing and laughing and crying all at once. She was so happy that she didn't know what to do.

"Tell me, Alek," she said, pulling back just far enough to look into his eyes. "However did you do it?"

"I had a lot of help," he replied. "Widow Zloto used her money to buy the supplies while I went looking for Summer Rose. After Prince Cynrik let me change the roses, your father and Dielle helped me collect them."

"My entire kingdom owes you a debt of gratitude," the prince said from the doorway as he entered the cottage. "There were many times when I knew we would not have won a battle if you hadn't told me what to do. The least I could do to repay you was to help your young man with your roses."

"We had just finished collecting them when word reached us that you had been kidnapped," said her father.

Alek hugged her tighter. His breath was warm on her cheek when he said, "After we learned that Zivon had you, we came as quickly as we could. Prince Cynrik wanted to bring Zivon back for trial, so we came together."

"I wondered why you were all here," said Serafina. "Thank you for everything!"

"You were the one who brought a giant to stop the fighting!" said Alek. "We'd still be at it if he hadn't stepped in. I never thought giants really existed or that I'd ever see one!"

"I've seen so many things that everyone said weren't real! When we get home, I have so much to tell everyone!"

"And we want to hear it all!" said her father. "Tell me, after seeing so many interesting places, where do you want to live?"

Serafina was trying to think of her answer when her mouth opened and she said in her Baba Yaga voice, "I will continue to live in my cottage as long as I am Baba Yaga. Even though I can regain my youth by drinking blue rose tea, the changes would be obvious. People like Zivon would seek me out and try to control me for their own benefit. I would be forced to move frequently and often without warning."

The moment she had started speaking as Baba Yaga, Serafina had slipped out of Alek's arms and backed away, a horrified look on her face. Her hand flew up to cover her mouth, and she shook her head as if to deny what she was saying.

Alek took a half step closer. "But I thought you would go back to being yourself if I brought you everything you asked for," he said in a quiet voice.

"I thought so, too!" said Serafina.

Alek moved another step closer. "You know that I love you and believe in you, right?"

Serafina nodded.

"So what else can I do?" Alek said, pleading for an answer.

"I don't know!" she replied, obviously distraught.

"If she is going to remain Baba Yaga, we must do something to ensure her safety," the prince interjected.

"What she just said was very true. Now that word about what Zivon did has gotten out, someone else is bound to try to exploit her for money. I can announce that she is under my protection, but that won't be effective unless she remains in my kingdom."

Alek gave Serafina a searching look before turning to speak to the prince. Suddenly, with so many people around, she felt as if there wasn't enough air in the cottage. Crossing her arms over her stomach as if to hold herself together, she ran outside, hoping to find someplace where she could be alone. When she saw how many people were milling around just beyond her gate, she left her yard and dashed into the forest, a sob caught in her throat.

"This isn't fair!" she cried out loud as she stumbled half unseeing through the underbrush. "I did everything I was supposed to do as Baba Yaga, and Alek did everything he could to help me. Why am I still Baba Yaga? I don't *want* to be Baba Yaga anymore! I want to be the girl I used to be!"

A shiver ran through Serafina, shaking her from head to toe. Even the trees seemed to feel it; their leaves fluttered as if a great wind had swept through the forest. Serafina thought she heard distant laughter, but she couldn't be sure. She looked around, expecting to see that someone had followed her, but no one was there. When a light rain began to fall, she closed her eyes and tilted her face to let the drops fall on her cheeks, her eyelids, and her lips. The water felt soothing on her skin, as if she'd been overheated. Then, as abruptly as it had started, the rain stopped. Serafina shuddered as something knotted inside her loosened. She felt as if a vital part of her had changed. Was it possible that the final thing she'd had to do to stop being Baba Yaga was to say what she wanted out loud?

"Fina!" Alek shouted from the cottage door. "Please come back! We need to talk."

Serafina had left the forest and was rounding the fence when a young page came running to find her. "The skull on your gate tried to bite me!" the boy complained. "It called me names and yelled at me, too."

"Did you do anything to the skull?" Serafina asked him.

The boy shrugged. "I tried to pick it up, that's all. I wasn't going to break it. I just wanted a better look. Why did it try to bite me like that?"

"He doesn't like being touched," said Serafina. "The first time I polished him, he—"

She realized with a start that the boy had asked her a question and she had answered it as herself, through her own personal experience, not in her Baba Yaga voice or with Baba Yaga's knowledge. And that could mean only one thing.

"I'm not Baba Yaga anymore!" she shouted as she ran to the cottage, her feet scarcely touching the ground. "Alek, did you hear me? I'm an ordinary girl again!"

"You were never ordinary!" Alek said, coming through the gate to pick her up and twirl her around.

"Wait," she said. "I'm sure it's true, but let's just make absolutely certain. You, squire!" she called to a passing young man dressed in the prince's livery. "Come over here and ask me a question! Make it something that no one could possibly answer."

"Okay," the squire said with a grin. "How many meat pies did my friend Josep steal from under the cook's nose last week?"

"I have no idea!" Serafina shouted, so happy that she took hold of Alek's hand and pulled him into a wild dance that made everyone laugh and start clapping out a rhythm. The soldiers who weren't watching the prisoners gathered close to see what was going on. Her father, the prince, and Dielle all came out of the cottage when they heard the uproar. Serafina and Alek danced until they were gasping for breath, but they didn't stop until it occurred to Serafina that there was something else that she needed to do.

"Dielle!" Serafina shouted, running to the girl and pulling her away from the others. "As far as I'm concerned, you *are* the next Baba Yaga. You may have become Baba Yaga when I gave up the job, but I want to make it official, just in case. I give my job to you! There, I said it," she announced, giving her friend a quick hug. "Let's see if it worked. We need a volunteer to ask Baba Yaga a question."

"Make it something that she won't know the answer to!" shouted the squire who had just asked Serafina a question.

"And make it a question that you really need answered," said Serafina. "Baba Yaga can answer only one question with the absolute truth for each person."

A soldier in the back of the crowd raised his hand. "I'll ask a question!" he shouted. "What are—"

"No, no, don't ask me!" Serafina cried. "Ask her," she told him, pointing at Dielle.

Everyone stepped aside as the soldier made his way to where Dielle and Serafina stood waiting. "I was adopted," he said when he stood before the girls. "No one knows the names of my real parents or why I was abandoned in a churchyard. My question is—why did my parents abandon me?"

"Your parents wanted to marry, but your mother's father refused to give them permission," Dielle said in the Baba Yaga voice. "They were fleeing their town when your mother gave birth to you. When her father came after them, he forced her to give you up. He was the one who left you in the churchyard. Your mother died soon after, but your birth father still lives. His name is Teodor Dlugosz."

The soldier was beaming by the time she finished. "I was sure my parents hadn't left me there because they didn't want me! Thank you so much! I've wanted to know the answer to that question my entire life."

"And Dielle was able to answer your question because she is the new Baba Yaga!" Serafina announced.

Dielle had looked surprised when she'd started talking in her Baba Yaga voice, but was even more startled when she looked down at her hem. "I've grown!" she cried. "Everything is shorter now. And tighter," she added, tugging at her collar.

"That will keep happening for a while," said Serafina. "There are clothes of different sizes in one of the trunks."

"If she really is the new Baba Yaga, you're finally

free, Serafina!" Alek said, an enormous grin spreading across his face. Drawing her into his arms, he spun her around, laughing, until they were both too dizzy to stand. They collapsed on the ground as everyone cheered.

"If we leave now," Alek told her, "I know of an inn we can reach before nightfall. We'll get to Prince Cynrik's castle tomorrow, then home three days later."

"That sounds wonderful," Serafina told him, "but I can't leave just yet. There are so many things I have to do first! I want to put things away and make sure every-thing is clean for the new Baba Yaga. Oh, I have to say good-bye to Maks and the skulls and the cottage. I'm going to miss them all so much! Promise me we can come visit them. I'll want to see Dielle and everyone as often as I can."

"Of course," said Alek. "Whenever you want. Did you say you're going to miss the skulls?"

Serafina nodded. "They're my friends, too. Maks and the skulls helped me when I was Baba Yaga, and the cottage rescued me I don't know how many times. I know that all I wanted was to be normal again, but I can't just walk away from my friends forever! And it's very important that I tell Dielle what her duties and responsibilities are, what she can and can't do, what to feed the cat, how to polish the skulls, and everything else I can think of that she needs to know. I have to tell her all the things that I wish someone had told me when I became Baba Yaga."

"Including how to pass the job on to someone else?" Alek asked, brushing his lips across hers.

"Especially that," she said.

Reaching up with one hand, Alek tilted her head back and kissed her with so much love that she felt her muscles go limp. It was the kiss she had been wanting for a very long time.

ACKNOWLEDGMENTS

My thanks to Grace Piskorski for helping me with Polish names and words, and to Serafina Rayner for lending me her first name.

In addition, I found my information about teas, including rose hip tea, in *Magic and Medicine of Plants*, by the editors of *Reader's Digest*, 1986.

Have you read all of E.D. Baker's magical stories?!

OUT NOW!